Heart Burn Holiday

I0618897

MICHELLE BUSBY

Patent Print Books
Panama City Beach, Florida

This is a work of fiction, and the views expressed herein are the sole responsibility of the author. The characters, places, and incidents portrayed in this book are products of the author's imagination, and any resemblance to actual persons, living or dead, or actual events or locales, is entirely coincidental.

<u>HEART BURN HOLIDAY</u>

Published by PATENT PRINT BOOKS
www.patentprintbks.com
PATENT PRINT BOOKS and the fingerprint colophon are registered trademarks of PATENT PRINT BOOKS

First Edition: 2022
Printed in the United States of America

ISBN 978-0-578-39462-6
Library of Congress Control Number: 2022

10   9   8   7   6   5   4   3   2   1

Dedicated to my children,
Who were the most difficult mysteries
I ever tried to solve,
And in memory of Zaccheus, Rascal, and Polo —
the real-life Zed, Red, and Sherlock.

In Appreciation

I want to express my appreciation for those who had a part in the inspiration and completion of this book: my publisher, my editor, my proofreaders, my fellow sleuths, my friends, and especially my family.

Introduction

"The history of every country begins in the heart of a man or a woman."

~ Willa Cather,
Pulitzer Prize winning American novelist
O Pioneers!

HAVE YOU EVER WONDERED what the celebration of *Cinco de Mayo* is all about and what significance it holds for America?

Popular belief marks May 5th as the celebration of Mexican Independence Day. That is a misconception. *Cinco de Mayo* is actually the celebration of one key Mexican battle victory—the *Battle of Puebla*—during which the French Empire was defeated.

After the Mexican American War of 1848 and the Reform War of 1861, the Mexican treasury was left bankrupted. President Benito Juárez announced his country would not be able to pay its foreign debt for two years.

Angered, the countries of Britain and Spain sailed to Veracruz to demand reimbursement. Realizing President Juárez had been truthful about the lack of funds, they peacefully negotiated a mutually satisfactory agreement and withdrew from Mexico.

France also sent naval forces to Veracruz, where Napoleon III sought to further France's interests by establishing what he called the "Second Mexican Empire."

The French fleet drove President Juárez and his government into retreat as they marched on toward Mexico City. At Fort Loreto and Fort Guadalupe near the town of Puebla, the French encountered unexpected resistance from a faction of 4,000 poorly equipped and bedraggled troops.

Under the leadership of a 33-year-old officer—General Ignacio Zaragoza—the small Mexican Army fought against the overconfident 8,000-man French forces. Zaragoza and his soldiers eventually defeated the French Army, thus giving a much-needed morale boost to the Mexican people.

The victory at Puebla was instrumental in engendering a surge of patriotism and establishing national unity throughout the country. President Juárez declared May 5th would be commemorated as a national holiday, called the "*Battle of Puebla Day*" or the "*Battle of Cinco de Mayo.*"

Sadly, General Zaragoza's victory was short-lived. He contracted typhoid fever and died only four months later. After less than a year, the French returned with an army of 30,000 and captured Mexico City. They set their own emperor, Maximilian I, to rule over the country.

In 1867, the United States offered military assistance to Mexico and with that help, Mexico was successful in removing the French influence. Maximilian I was executed, and Benito Juárez was returned to office as Mexico's President.

Historians speculate that, had Mexico not defeated the initial French attempt to take over at the *Battle of Puebla*, France would have come to the aid of the American Confederacy, and the American Civil War would likely have had a different outcome.

Though May 5ᵗʰ is no longer observed as a national holiday in Mexico, all public schools in the country are closed in observance, and in the State of Puebla, it remains an official holiday that is celebrated with food, festivals, parades, fireworks, and historical reenactments.

What's all that have to do with tea and potions? According to Tommie Watson, any day is a good day to celebrate a victory with tea. *¡Viva la revolución de té!*

~ *Michelle Busby*

Chapter One

"Is your mama a llama?" I asked my friend Llyn.
"Oh, Lloyd, don't be silly!" Llyn said with a grin.
"My mama has big ears, long lashes and fur ...
And you, of all people should know about her!
Our mamas belong to the same herd, and you
know all about llamas, 'cause you are one, too!"
~Deborah Guarino, Steven Kellogg,
Is Your Mama a Llama?

TWELVE HOURS. WHAT CAN HAPPEN IN TWELVE HOURS?

On Monday, May 5, 1862, the Mexican Army fought from daybreak to dusk against a foreign enemy. When night fell, they had defeated the French forces at the *Battle of Puebla*. They suffered 83 fatalities.

On Sunday, May 5, 2019, Mexican Americans in the town of Greenleaf, Florida, celebrated *Cinco de Mayo*

from daybreak to dusk and into the night with music, feasting, drinking, dancing, and fireworks. When night fell, a battle was raged against a common enemy. Floral county suffered three fatalities—noted cardiologist Dr. Norman Frank, pharmacist Larry Clay, and local runaround Jimmy Clay—all apparent victims of massive heart attacks.

What can happen in twelve hours? Controversial cardiac casualties.

Chapter Two

THOMASINA "TOMMIE" WATSON leaned on her teal-colored cane as she limped back and forth in front of her *Dos Más Dos Taquitos* booth, waiting for Detective Earl Petry to arrive on the scene. Once again, she was in the middle of suspicious deaths—this time a triple!

Thankfully, Tommie's street food booth was far away from Watson's Reme-Teas, her herbal teas and potions shop in downtown Floribunda, Florida. Nevertheless, she found herself directly at the forefront of the tragedy at the combination *Cinco de Mayo* event and double engagement party. To make matters worse, she had absolutely no clue what happened.

The day had started out pleasantly when residents of Floral County and out-of-town visitors gathered on Main Street in Greenleaf to celebrate the two special occasions—the Mexican Army's 1862 victory over the

French Empire at the *Battle of Puebla* and the engagements of Santino Alvarez to Jo Clay and Leo Alvarez to Elly James. As the partying crowd meandered through the street singing, dancing, congratulating the happy couples, and sampling the traditional Mexican American dishes from the *cabinas* of the local vendors, other battles ensued: People ate a lot, and some folks drank too much. Arguments surfaced, but like the fireworks, most fizzled after the initial explosions. The Alvarez brothers caught plenty of good-natured ribbing, but they took it well, and, for the most part, everyone got along without incident ... until Jimmy Clay arrived.

Jimmy was the very definition of a lowlife. He was a troublemaker, a reprobate, and a scoundrel, but a darn good-looking one, with electric blue eyes peering beneath thick dark lashes, muscular arms, and dimples in a tanned face that women couldn't seem to resist. To be sure, one could find several children around Floral County with similar eyes and dimples.

A seemingly minor scuffle broke out between Jimmy and Santino Alvarez, who was marrying Jimmy's ex-wife Jo Clay. A single punch was thrown, and suddenly, three Floribunda men—including Jimmy—were dead. The bodies lay on the street in front of the food booths manned by Tommie and her friend, Finbar Holmes. Already, she could hear the whispers and see the furtive glances in their direction. *Dangitall,* she thought, *here we go again!*

The noise in the street continued, but the tone had

undergone subtle changes. Raucous laughter had dissolved into short self-conscious tittering as the celebrants tried to make light of the sobering situation. Children still ran around and played, but their jubilant exultations were more subdued, and mothers and grandmothers frequently shushed them. The *mariachi* band members sat on the edge of the raised platform they used as a stage, nervously smoking, and drinking *cervesas*, their instruments cast aside as they gulped the cold beers.

In the center of the thoroughfare, Simone Lorence and Katherine Clay—their faces white and tear-stained—stood away from the table beneath which their loved ones lay. The bodies of two of the dead men had been cordoned off by Padre Sanchez, Finbar Holmes, Don Lareby, and Henry Erving, holding two brightly colored tablecloths between them to shield Norman Frank and Larry Clay from view. A bit farther down the street, a few men from the congregation of the Catholic church, *Iglesia de Santa Maria*, huddled around Jimmy Clay in an effort to protect his body from lookie-loos, but the surge of the crowd ebbed around all three deceased men like the current of a lazy river.

Tommie Watson noticed the food *cabinas* continued to have a steady stream of customers. *What is it about the proximity to death that makes people hungry?* she wondered.

A pewter grey unmarked police SUV caught her attention as it pulled up and stopped before the wooden barricade that kept pedestrians safe from vehicles. The

driver's side door opened, and the car visibly lifted as the occupant stepped out. Tommie could almost imagine the springs creaking. To her credit, she didn't giggle and snort—something she often did when under duress.

The driver was a large, muscular man with short, cropped silver hair and a neatly trimmed white mustache and beard accentuating his strong, square jaw. He stood and surveyed the scene while his partner exited the vehicle.

She was a perfect contrast—a tall, fit young woman with tiny features, her wavy light brown hair pinned back in a low ponytail. Officer Jenny Foran wore the traditional khaki and hunter green Floribunda Police Department uniform; Detective Earl Petry was more casually dressed, with khaki slacks and a lighter green button-down shirt with the sleeves rolled up to his elbows and the collar open, revealing the tips of curly white hair on his barrel chest. The crowd buzzed excitedly and hastened to clear a path as the two skirted the barricade and walked toward the tables.

Detective Earl Petry looked directly at Tommie Watson and let out a deep sigh.

"Tommie," he said, his voice a low baritone.

"Earl," Tommie replied in her alto register.

They stood unmoving for several beats, and then he turned toward his partner and nodded.

"Jenny, watch over those two bodies, please. Here comes Dale." He lifted his chin toward a marked patrol car arriving on the scene. "As soon as Sanderson gets here, you and Dale can start taking statements."

A tall and lanky young officer sauntered up to them. Dale Dicenza, at six foot one, was an inch shorter than the older man and a good 40 pounds lighter, baby-faced, with light blond hair and pale blue eyes. He nodded in Tommie's direction.

"Hey, Ms. Watson," he said.

"Hi, Dale," Tommie answered.

"Earl, where do you want me?" Dale asked.

"Go guard that one in the street. Wait, Sandy's here. Never mind. Go with Jenny and get statements."

Earl stepped forward, took Tommie by the elbow, and guided her toward the prone body of Jimmy Clay. She limped along without comment. As they approached the throng of men surrounding the deceased, the big detective smiled and nodded.

"Thank you, fellas. *Gracias.* Appreciate your help."

The guardians shook his hand and dispersed, many gravitating toward the food booths. Again, Tommie wondered why death stimulated appetite.

Looking beyond Detective Petry, she saw the coroner and his three assistants. Sanderson Harper—Tommie's cousin—was 63, with dark graying hair, black frame glasses, and a decided middle age spread. He cast a look in her direction and shook his head. She shrugged.

As two of the assistants came over and secured the body of Jimmy Clay, Earl Petry directed Tommie to a picnic table and sat her down backwards on the bench, helping her lift her outstretched left leg so she could rest it

on the seat. He pulled a chair facing her and straddled it. Then, he reached forward and took her hands, his steely blue-grey eyes staring into her chocolate brown ones.

"Darlin', are you all right?"

"I'm a little shaken up, Earl, but I'm OK."

"I guess you are! What the hell, Tommie? Three dead men? What happened here?"

"I don't know. I honestly don't know. One minute everyone was eating and drinking and having a ball. The next thing I know, Jo shouted, then Santino Alvarez punched Jimmy Clay in the face and knocked him out. Larry Clay stood up at the table and looked toward his brother, then he fell over, and his wife screamed. Dr. Frank began to perform CPR, but he started puking and had to quit. Gertrudis Padilla gave the doctor a potion and settled him back in his chair. Then, Dr. Frank just kicked over backwards and died." Her eyes were wide and tear-filled.

Earl squeezed her hands gently. "Did you …?"

"No! I was nowhere near any of them until Dr. Frank collapsed. I started CPR, but he was already dead. I served them some food, but that was way earlier, and Simone and Katherine ate the same food, and so did I."

Earl smiled at her urgently sincere face. "Darlin', this is a doozy for sure. I'm gonna let Dale and Jenny take your statement, just for the record, but I wanted to make sure you're OK."

"No. You wanted to make sure I'm not involved in this. I'm absolutely not, and nobody can point a finger at

me ... *this time.*" She emphasized the last two words.

Earl choked off a laugh, which would have been highly inappropriate in the current situation. Instead, he pulled her to her feet and, in the process of leaning over, planted a quick kiss on her cheek. "C'mon, Ziggy. Let's get you and your bad luck storm cloud back to your partner-in-crime, the illustrious detective Holmes. I'm sure you two have lots of notes to compare. Just do me a favor and stay out of trouble. OK? It's exhausting trying to keep my woman alive and well!"

Chapter Three

FINBAR HOLMES surrendered the tablecloth he held to the coroner and his assistant, and then he joined his friends Don and Henry off to the side of the road as officers Foran and Dicenza interrogated Padre Sanchez. *The game's afoot again,* he thought, pursing his thin lips.

Finbar ran his hand through his sparse, light brown hair and scratched the side of one of his half-moon shaped ears as he watched Tommie and Earl talking down the street. He wished he could hear their conversation. No doubt Earl was giving her his standard warning against investigating and interviewing witnesses, and no doubt Tommie would not comply. This was the third time Finbar and Tommie had been involved in what turned out to be murder, and he was relatively sure it wouldn't be the last.

Finbar Holmes was a retired Inspector for the

Food Safety Authority of Ireland. He had been an FSAI Inspector for many years until his wife Mary died of cancer. At 66 he became a pensioner. At 71, with his four children grown and with children of their own, he set out in pursuit of what he planned as his last home.

In February, he up and left his terrace house in Dublin and moved to the States. Finbar was a sun worshipper who relished in tanning his pale Irish skin to a most unnatural shade of brown. He regularly took holidays to locations like Spain, Portugal, or the Canary Islands but had grown increasingly tired of the damp, dreary periods in between which caused his tan to fade.

He had scoured the internet looking for a warm, sunny location to live—away from the cold and rainy climate in Ireland. He happened upon a sales advertisement for a duplex in Floribunda, Florida. Finding the name quaint and the price reasonable, he wired the agents at Floral Real Estate and bought the building, sight unseen. Thereafter, he packed up his belongings, had them shipped to Florida, and flew to America with his emotional support dog, Sherlock, to become Floribunda's newest residents.

Upon his arrival, he found the duplex lacking in what he considered the necessary conveniences of home. He had immediately set about redecorating and refurbishing the unoccupied unit to suit his tastes. At the time, he intended to utilize the entire duplex for himself and his dog.

A woman lived in the A-unit who had two medium-sized dogs of her own, which he could hear

through the connecting wall. She was 64, just barely over five feet tall, and weighed in the neighborhood of 200 pounds or so—a good 70 pounds more than he carried on his wiry 5'7" frame. She often played the piano and sang to her pups, which Finbar could hear through the wall, and he noted she had a much better than average voice. She kept her mostly salt and some pepper hair cut short in a pixie style, which suited her personality and complemented the dimples in her pudgy face.

On his first meeting with Thomasina Watson and her dogs Zed and Red, he noted the congeniality of her pets and their immediate attachment to Sherlock.

"Halloo!" he had called when she brought her boys out the back door into the garden where he was sunbathing. "How're ye doin', missus? I'm yer neighbor."

The woman had stumbled backwards at the sight of his hairy, half naked body.

"I'm … I'm Thomasina Watson, but people call me Tommie. Please, don't evict me," she had blurted.

Finbar had decided right then and there to keep her as his neighbor. Over the next weeks, he and Thomasina had become fast friends. They both shared an interest in animals, food, puzzles, and mysteries. At first, he thought she must work in a medical field, for she wore hospital scrubs in all colors and patterns. He later learned that she favored them because they had an abundance of pockets, and the loose pants fit over the heavy black walking boot she wore as a result of a broken ankle suffered in Florida's

category five hurricane Adam the previous October.

Tommie Watson was a recent newcomer to Floribunda, as well. The only person in town she knew was her cousin, Sanderson Harper, who was the county coroner and who owned a sandwich shop on Bottlebrush Boulevard, the main street through the town. Tired of the sandwich side business, Sandy rented the space to Thomasina for her herbal teas and potions shop called Watson's Reme-Teas—a name Holmes thought well suited for the retired schoolteacher turned certified herbalist.

Finbar subsequently bought the lease on Tommie's herbal shop, as well as that of an adjoining space which had been a booming morning coffee business. An amateur chef, he sold Irish coffee during the week and conducted cooking demonstrations on the weekend in the intimate 20-seat "restaurant" he named *Caife Caife Holmes,* which was Gaelic for Holmes's Coffee Café.

When a woman named Coral Beadwell collapsed and died on the floor of Tommie's shop, he and his new neighbor/friend/tenant put their heads together to solve the crime using a detailed process Finbar had devised for unraveling mystery shows on television. The method was successful, and the two of them cracked the woman's murder and that of the agent who sold Holmes the duplex.

Thereafter, they and their small circle of friends took to calling themselves "Holmes and Watson, Investigators," modeled after the legendary Sherlock Holmes and Dr. Watson team made famous in Sir Arthur

Conan Doyle's mystery novels. They had recently solved another set of murders the past April when a woman named Veranell Collins was killed during the annual Easter Egg Hide and Charity Raffle.

Both investigations had resulted in attempts on Finbar's and Tommie's lives. Detective Earl Petry, Tommie's boyfriend, had done his best to deter the duo from embarking on their investigative efforts, but Tommie was a stubborn and independent woman whose tenacity matched that of Holmes, himself. In the end, even Earl had to admit they were unusually successful in their methods, and he had reluctantly allowed them to continue with their amateur sleuthing, knowing full well he had to keep a close watch to prevent them from getting themselves killed.

Now, with three men dropping dead one after the other, Finbar was certain foul play was involved, and he could scarcely wait to corner Thomasina and get her take on the deaths.

"Halloo, Detective," Finbar said.

"Hey there, Holmes. I'm putting this woman into your custody while I help Dale and Jenny conduct interviews. Will you see that she stays put and doesn't get into any trouble?" Earl said.

"I can't make ye any promises. You know her mind better than anyone. I can only tell ye that I'll do m'best."

Earl scoffed. "That's all I can hope for, Holmes. Look, will you two at least wait until after we've done our initial interviews before you start mucking up the works?"

Tommie scowled but remained quiet. Finbar, Don, and Henry all laughed heartily, which made her scowl even more. She sat down heavily in a chair vacated by Don. Earl leaned over and smoothed her hair.

"Tommie …"

"Earl …"

"Lord, woman. Please. I'm begging you. I can't tell you not to get involved, but please, please be careful. That goes for you, too, Finbar."

"As ye say, Earl. 'Twill be difficult with this one, but I'll give it m'best effort."

"Thanks. And the same goes for you guys," Earl said to Don and Henry, "and Elaine and Susan, too."

Don Lareby gulped and fidgeted, casting furtive glances at his friend Henry Erving. The two men constituted one-half of what Tommie and Finbar called the "Fab Four." The other half was comprised of Don's twin sisters, Elaine Frank and Susan Clay. The four of them were gossips extraordinaire, and they knew more about the residents of Floral County than the residents knew about themselves. Their information was a keystone of the Holmes and Watson investigations.

"We will, Earl," Henry said.

At 61, Henry was the same height as the burly detective and 15 pounds lighter, but Earl's 210 pounds were all muscle, while Henry held his weight in his paunch. He had been the boyfriend of two of the women for whom Tommie and Finbar had solved the murders, and he had

been an early suspect. After being cleared, he was "adopted" by Don's sisters, both of whom vied for his affections.

Hearing their names, the sisters hurriedly made their way to the group. Both women were 45, stood the same height as Holmes, but weighed the same as Tommie. They were impossible to tell apart, except for the clothing they wore, which only differed in color. Their brother Don was 41 and slender. All three siblings had light brown hair and identical amber eyes.

"Hey, Earl," the women called in unison.

"Ladies. I was just telling Don and Henry I want the four of you to mind your Ps and Qs. I know you'll be digging up dirt, but don't forget that cats don't like it when you scratch in their litter boxes."

The women giggled and nodded, taking up flanking positions on either side of Henry.

Earl cast his eyes around at the six of them and slowly shook his head. "Hopeless, ain't it? I know exactly what y'all are gonna do. Just be careful and be sure to keep me in the loop the entire time," he begged.

"Don't you worry, Earl. We'll be particular," Don said. "Won't we sisters?"

"Oh, for cripes sake, Donnie. We know what he means," Elaine said.

Susan snickered. "We'll watch out for Tommie."

Earl sighed again, leaned over, kissed the top of Tommie's head, and ambled off in the direction of his officers, leaving Holmes and Watson, Investigators, and the

Fab Four already with their heads together discussing the deaths of the three men.

Chapter Four

TOMMIE WATSON scanned the crowd illuminated by the hazy yellow light of the strung-up bulbs running down either side of Main Street between the two wooden barricades. Three of the long rectangular tables and chairs lining the center of the street were occupied by the food vendors who were waiting for their turns to be questioned by Earl and his officers. The others held mostly curious onlookers and elderly men and women who had tired of walking around.

Sandy's assistants had already encased the bodies of Norman Frank, Larry Clay, and Jimmy Clay in black body bags and loaded them into the back of the medical examiner's SUV for transport to the morgue. Now that the corpses were removed, the remaining crowd resumed their activities. The fireworks display had been cut short, but

nobody was in the mood to shoot off any more of them. Several street food booths, however, still served patrons.

After their four nosy friends left them, Finbar had offered to pack up Tommie's food, so she sat on her chair and cast her eyes in a line from the first booth to the last on the opposite street, looking at their signs and recalling the dishes served by their vendors.

At *Cabina* I, León Luz served *Chips de Tortilla Fritos.* The deep-fried tortilla chips had been crispy and were the delivery system for many of the sauces offered by other vendors.

León's wife Letitia manned the next *cabina* where she sold *Queso Fundido Picante Salsa*—spicy white cheese sauce. She graciously gave Tommie a quart-sized mason jar full of the sauce to take home.

The gossipy sisters shared a larger double tent next to Letitia. They sold two items prepared by the brides-to-be. Santino's fiancé Jo Clay made *Salsa Roja Sedosa* and called it Jo's Silky Red Sauce and Leo's fiancé Elly James made *Salsa en Copas*, a layered sauce presented in quilted jelly jars from her shop, Elly's Jelly Jar.

The next booth served *Pico de Gallo Fresco*. Lara Padilla, a young woman in her mid-20s, manned the booth, and her vivacious eight-year-old daughter Dearci served the fresh vegetable sauce to the customers in tiny bowls she had fashioned at Jo Clay's ceramics shop, The Clay Pigeon.

Directly across from Tommie's *cabina* was the tent occupied by Lara's mother, Gertrudis Padilla. The

sign at the top read *Remedios de Hierbas*—Herbal Remedies. Mrs. Padilla was well known in the town of Greenleaf for her natural herbal medicines. Her tent functioned as the first aid station for the party and even had two narrow cots set up at the back for celebrants who needed to rest and recover.

Tommie had spent the morning chatting with Gertrudis, comparing herbal potions and preparation techniques. She was delighted to learn Gertrudis used herbs frown in her own garden. Her concoctions for the celebration covered only three conditions, but the preparations treated nearly all the ailments one would imagine occurring during the event. They included: *Para el Vientre: Indigestión, Náuseas, o Dolor de Estómago* (For the Belly: Indigestion, Nausea, or Stomachache); *Para la Cabeza: Embriaguez, Resaca, o Dolor de Cabeza* (For the Head: Drunkenness, Hangover, or Headache); and *Para el Corazán: Acidez o Reflujo Ácido* (For the Heart: Heartburn or Acid Reflux). Tommie enjoyed "talking shop" and sharing recipes with the woman, who was near her own age. The two of them had hit it off immediately.

The booth next to Gertrudis was a double tent and was run by pharmacist Hector Flores and his wife, Carmine. Their specialty was a mouth-watering pork tamales recipe handed down through their family for generations—*Tamales Carnitas Flores*.

The Ladies of *Iglesia de Santa Maria* ran the next booth, which was also a double sized tent. They served *Empanadas de Pollo*—chicken empanadas. They also manned the adjacent single booth of *Refrescas Frios*—cold soft drinks which were all Mexican brands.

Directly across from the soft drink booth, on the opposite side of the cordoned off street, was a single tent which sold *Cervezas Helados*. The Men of *Iglesia de Santa Maria* dispensed the iced beer at that tent, as well as the double tent beside it which featured the well-liked *Churros de Canela*—cinnamon churros.

Jorge and Soledad Fuentes occupied the next *cabina* where they sold delicious *Sopes de Ternera con Frijoles Negros*—beef tortillas with black beans.

Tommie's booth was the next in line, and she had two items for sale. She named the booth *Dos Más Dos Taquitos*—Two Plus Two Taquitos. The first taquito dish she offered was *Cerdo con Queso*—cheesy pulled pork, and the second was *Pollo con Salsa Verde*—chicken with green sauce.

To the left of Tommie's booth was a double tent shared by Don Lareby and Henry Erving. The Alvarez brothers had provided a delicious dry meat beef jerky they called *Carne Seca de Alvarez*, which was sold by Don, and Henry had prepared skewered corn on the cob coated in mayonnaise and cheese called *Elotes en Brochetas*.

Finbar's booth, which was the next double tent, was probably the most popular of the dessert items, and his food was cooked on the spot. He sautéed fresh bananas in butter, dusted them with cinnamon, and drizzled sweetened condensed milk on top. The *Platanos con Lechera* were served piping hot on small paper plates.

The final *cabina* was run by Padre Juan Sanchez, the priest at *Iglesia de Santa Maria*. Other than the drinks, his items were the only store-bought treats. The *Caramelos de Tamarindo*—an assortment of candies sweetened with tamarind—were a favorite of the

children, and he gave them to the kids free of charge.

Finbar walked up next to Tommie and rested his hand on the back of her chair, causing her to flinch.

"I'm sorry to startle ye, missus, but are ye nearly ready to go home? I've boxed yer leftovers and put them in the boot of yer auto. Will ye be using them for yer Mother's Day luncheon on Sunday next?"

"No, Finbar. I'm making tea sandwiches. I hope tonight's fiasco doesn't keep people from attending."

"Ach. I'm sure yer mammies and babbies will come. They've no part of this misadventure."

"You're probably right. Anyhow, Earl said we could leave as soon as we were questioned, and we have been, so let's us go on home. I'm tired, and my ankle is killing me. He'll be here for a while longer." She flexed her left foot, which had been elevated on another chair.

"Righto." Finbar extended his hand and helped her to her feet.

Tommie clutched the brightly colored aluminum cane Finbar had given her as a present when she finally came out of the walking boot. She stood still a moment to stabilize herself, painfully aware of the throbbing in her ankle. Though the surgery had been successful, and the pins, screws, and plate held the healing bone in place, the ankle would never be 100%, due in part to her age, weight, and nerve damage from the severity of the break.

She took a step and winced from the pain. Finbar grasped her more firmly by the elbow and escorted her past the barricade. Just before she got in the car, Tommie took a quick look back and was rewarded with an air kiss from Earl as he watched her leave the grounds.

Chapter Five

EARL PETRY watched Tommie and Finbar pull away into traffic and felt a familiar knot in his stomach. He dreaded the coming days, knowing Holmes and Watson would begin their unofficial investigation. He could only guess what trouble they'd get themselves into. His protection instincts kicked in, and he already worried about Tommie.

Earl had been born and raised in Floral County. Married and divorced twice, he vowed he would never tie the knot again. A tall, handsome, well-built man in a town where eligible bachelors were in short supply, he had his pick and choice for partners; there were plenty of females wanting to be the third Mrs. Petry. He dated many but fell for none … until Tommie Watson moved to town.

He had met Tommie briefly when she first arrived in Floribunda in January of 2019. At that time, she was still

in a wheelchair after suffering a broken ankle from a fall following the devastating hurricane that destroyed much of Bay City, Floribunda, Riverton, and many neighboring inland towns. He had stopped by on his rounds to check out the woman who had taken over the coroner's shop, Sandy's Sandwiches.

He found the herbalist pulling her wheelchair along with one foot and coasting through the store, busily cleaning the round tables, sweeping the floor, and singing. The door was propped open, so the overhead bell didn't jingle. Earl stood in the doorway and just observed, amazed as she efficiently propelled herself from one place to the next, belting out an opera song playing on her CD. When she finally spotted him, she stopped singing, waved, and let out a peeling laugh that ended with a snort.

I think that's when I was hooked, Earl decided. After that first encounter, Tommie Watson was the only woman Earl wanted.

As a three-time divorcee, Tommie was also anti-marriage. That suited Earl fine. She was 64; he was 58. The difference in age was negligible, in Earl's eyes. Her weight was a non-issue, too. Earl liked his women "fluffy." Theirs was a steady, monogamous relationship without the entanglements of a legal contract. The whole town knew they were an item, but Tommy and Earl were discreet about the personal details of their courtship. They maintained a standing date for dinner each Wednesday night, with frequent meetups during the weekdays, but no overnight

sleepovers yet. They scrupulously avoided the L-word, but the feeling between them was entirely mutual.

"Earl, I think we're done here," Jenny said from behind him.

Earl nodded but didn't turn around. His eyes still followed the taillights of Tommie's RAV4.

"Good work, Jenny."

Jenny moved up and stood at his shoulder, casting her eyes in the direction he gazed.

"She'll be all right, Earl. Dale and I will double our drive-by surveillance of her house and shop."

The big detective turned to face his partner. "I appreciate that, Jenny." He let out a sigh. "I've never known a woman to get in the middle of so much trouble."

Jenny laughed and clapped him on the back lightly. "Yep. She's a horse of a different color, for sure, but she's much more refreshing than some of your other lady friends in the past. Don't worry. We'll keep a sharp eye out."

"Keep a sharp eye out for what ... or who?" Dale asked as he joined them. Getting silent eye rolls from Jenny, he opened his mouth and nodded. "Ah, gotcha. You mean Ms. Watson. We better keep both eyes out for her."

Earl grunted in reply. "What's the take on the statements ya'll have gotten so far?"

"Hanged if I know," Dale said, tilting his hat back on his head a bit. "It appears they all had heart attacks or something. Nobody really saw much, except for a squabble between Jo Clay and her ex-husband, Jimmy. And then

Santino Alvarez defended her by knocking the ex out. It was just one punch, from what everybody says. Not a beat down by any means. And Clay was already pretty drunk."

"Dr. Frank and Jimmy's brother, Larry, both died at the table. According to the witnesses, they went down just like they'd been shot, but, of course, there were no gunshots," Jenny said.

"But several people said they thought they heard shots fired," Dale said.

"Fireworks were going off right about that time, so I think the witnesses were confused," Jenny observed.

"Mm-hm," Earl mumbled. "Healthy men don't just up and keel over dead from fireworks or loud noises, not like this, and not without preexisting conditions. Head on back to the station and file your reports, then go on home. I'm gonna visit Sandy and see if he can expedite the autopsies. I'll see y'all in the morning."

As Jenny and Dale left in Dale's patrol car, Earl turned around in a circle and surveyed the scene on Main Street. Vendors bustled about quietly in various stages of packing up their food, while a crew of helpers began dismantling the tents and sweeping up the street. In a matter of an hour or so, there would be no trace of the *Cinco de Mayo* celebration, but it would be much longer before the town of Greenleaf would be back to normal.

Chapter Six

TOMMIE AND FINBAR arrived at the duplex and entered her unit. She opened the refrigerator, and he stacked the leftovers snugly inside. Red, the wiry-haired Portuguese Podengo Pequeño, danced about on his back legs, barking excitedly, and Zed, the brindle Boston Terrier, hopped in place on all fours. Tommie reached down and patted both of them on the head.

"Chill out, boys. I'm home now," she cooed.

"I hear m'mate Sherlock next door expressing his displeasure for leaving him in the dark so long. I'm going over, missus. Will ye be coming along for a nightcap and some conversation, or are ye too tired?" Finbar said.

"I'm tired, but I'll be over in just a minute. Gonna change into some different shoes first. Why don't you get the tea kettle on?"

"Could use a sup m'self. Not much in the mood for a Guinness. Have ye any of that *Dreamer Creamer*? I've used all of mine."

"Take me just a jiffy to whip some up. See you in a bit. Go ahead with Finbar, boys."

The dogs dutifully followed Finbar out the kitchen door while their mistress combined the makings for the creamer: eight ounces of fresh whole milk, a tablespoon of rose water, and half a teaspoon of freshly ground nutmeg. She made her way to the bedroom, kicked off her flat-heeled mules, and slipped her feet into a pair of well-worn Crocs. Grasping the container of creamer from the counter, she stepped onto the back patio, turned left, and turned left again, directly through Finbar's kitchen door.

"Good timing, lad. The kettle's already singing," he said, covering it with a knitted daffodil cozy and bringing it to the table.

Tommie smiled. He called men, women, children, and pets "lad." She took her usual seat and gratefully accepted a full cup of the steaming Barry's Irish tea. She added a generous dollop of honey and took a sip.

"Mmm. Nothing like a cup of tea to take away the stresses of the day."

Finbar poured a dash of the creamer into his oversized mug before adding tea. A longtime diabetic, he did not take any sweetener.

"Ah, that's lovely. I had a throat." That was his way of saying he was thirsty. It had taken Tommie a while to

fully understand the nuances of his Irish dialect and occasional odd turn of phrase.

"OK. While we decompress, will you tell me what in holy heck happened today? Three men dead, and I am thoroughly perplexed, Finbar."

"I'm confused m'self, lad. 'Twas a quare strange evening, sure. From my point of view, nothing out of the ordinary occurred except for Santino boxing that Clay man's nose. The two at the table just tumbled over. I've never seen anything like it."

"I observed Jimmy Clay trailing after Jo when she walked toward the soft drink stand. And earlier, there was some sort of drama going on at the salsa booth where the little girl was helping her mother. Did you notice that?"

"I heard their voices sounding angry, but I didn't see it. Tell me what ye saw."

Tommie leaned back in her chair and took another swig of tea. "Jo went to the booth. The little girl ... her name's Dearci ... she ran around and hugged Jo. Gertrudis said the child makes a lot of ceramic things in Jo's shop, and she's really fond of her. She crafted the tiny, flowered bowls they served the *pico de gallo* in. Anyway, Jo's ex-husband sauntered up and put his hand on Jo's shoulder. She shrugged it off and gave him a glare and told him to leave her alone, but he laughed and grabbed her again. Then, he leaned down and said something to Dearci. Jo got really ticked off when he reached out and touched the little girl's face. And so did Lara, her mother. She spouted off

something at him and pulled her daughter back."

"What'd he say?"

"I don't know. Fireworks were popping, and I couldn't hear their words, but whatever it was, it made both Jo and Lara really mad. The child just looked confused. Then I saw Jimmy lunge at Jo. Jo snatched her hand away and her salsa bowl hit the counter. The bowl cracked, and Dearci started to cry. Jimmy picked up the broken bowl and drank the sauce right out of it. It was loud. I could actually hear the slurping from across the road. It was so gross."

"Disgusting lout. What then?"

"He put his nasty hand on Jo's butt! I couldn't believe my eyes. She slapped him in the face, and he laughed and staggered to the table where his brother and Dr. Frank were sitting with Simone and Katherine."

"Did ye not see Santino with his fiancé during that time at all, Thomasina?"

"I did. Santino appeared at Jo's side just after she slapped Jimmy. He got in Jimmy's face, but Jo pulled him away. Later on, he and Jo caught up with Leo and Elly at the sisters' booth. It was a while afterwards that I saw Jimmy Clay stalking Jo again when she went for drinks. He had his hands on her waist, and she was shouting and struggling to get away. Then, Santino and Leo ran up to them. Leo pulled Jimmy Clay off Jo, and Santino drew back his fist and socked Jimmy right in the jaw. It knocked the man off his feet. He lifted up about a foot before he came crashing down on the street."

"Did he now? Yer man's got a strong arm!"

"I'll say! Leo held Santino back and kept him from hitting Jimmy again. The next thing I knew, Jo was sobbing and crying in Santino's arms. Some men from the beer tent hurried up and knelt over Jimmy. I distinctly heard the word *'muerto'* several times. That means dead."

"Aye. 'Tis exactly what it means. Do ye remember what came next?"

"Uh-huh. Larry Clay jumped up from his seat like he was gonna go there, but then he just careened over and smashed his face on the table before crumpling to the ground. Katherine screamed his name again and again. It gave me flashbacks to Coral Beadwell dropping dead in my shop back in February."

"Sure, sure. That'll come to yer mind often enough. What about the other man? Dr. Frank?"

"He saw Larry fall and went to him and began CPR, but then he started vomiting, and his girlfriend Simone started hollering. Gertrudis ran from her booth and administered a couple of potions to the doctor. She helped him back to his chair, but suddenly he flipped over backwards. I got there quick as I could and tried to give him CPR, but he was already dead."

"That's what I remember, too. Their table was right in front of me. The chemist stood up and seemed to capsize, landing face down. The doctor worked on him, got sick, and Mrs. Padilla poured some tonics into him. After they sat him back down, the doctor's chair upturned with

him in it. The two younger women screamed. From my perspective, which was a bit different than yers, there was nobody nearby to interfere with them before you went over to work on the doctor. Nobody even looked their way. Most of the crowd were watching the altercation at the end of the street. I didn't see Santino punch the man because Henry was bending over serving some customers. My eyes was directed straight ahead."

"Could you hear anything they said at the table before or after the fight?"

"Nah. There was too much noise all around. I could see their faces right well, though. Mr. Clay looked anxious, even before he stood up to see the fight. His wife's face was red. They both looked angry. I think they may have been having a row. He kept fidgeting with the bottle of beer on the table in front of him. When he jumped up, the beer splashed all on his shirt."

"Hmm. What about Dr. Frank?"

"Ah! Our friend Elaine's ex-husband. He looked a might pasty-faced when he arrived. His live-in girlfriend and he appeared to be on the outs. 'Twas not a congenial group, for sure. He never looked up when the argument occurred between Ms. Jo Clay's former and future husbands. The doctor seemed shocked when his chemist mate collapsed, though. 'Twas mere seconds after he drank that woman's potions before he fell over dead."

"Dangit, Finbar! This is so bizarre! It reminds me too much of Veranell Collins dying in the gazebo on Easter

Sunday. I'm glad I wasn't the one dispensing the herbal tonic this time!"

"M'self as well, lad. All ye did was pump the man's chest. I don't know what happened, but I can guarantee ye it was foul play. At least one, if not all three of them chaps was purposely killed."

"Agreed." Tommie paused a moment, then she leaned forward and tapped on the table. "Finbar, I just realized something very odd about the men who died."

"Odder than the fact they each died of unknown causes on the same night at nearly the same time?"

"Yeah. More than the *what, when, how,* and *why* of the deaths, there's a curious link as to the *who* that died."

"Elaborate, please, dear Watson."

"Blood and relations. Think. Jimmy Clay. Larry Clay. Norman Frank. Where's the commonality?"

Holmes put his slender finger to his pursed lips and frowned. Then, his eyes widened.

"Jayze! I see it! Jimmy Clay, formerly married to yer friend, Jo Clay. His brother, Larry Clay, formerly married to our friend, Susan Clay ..."

"And Dr. Norman Frank, formerly married to Susan's sister and our friend, Elaine Frank. My brain's too tired tonight to mull it over, but tomorrow, I say we get started on our investigation."

"What about yer Detective Petry, missus?"

Tommie fluttered her eyelashes. "Earl didn't tell me *not* to investigate. He only told me to be careful."

Finbar rolled his eyes dramatically and scoffed. "Don't count on it, Thomasina."

Chapter Seven

EARL PETRY sat in a worn leather chair in Sanderson Harper's office on Monday morning, his long legs crossed at the ankles, nursing a cup of hot coffee while waiting for the coroner to join him. He yawned. His watch read 8:05, and he knew Sandy had been in since 6:00 that morning, attending to the autopsies of the three DOAs from Greenleaf after staying late the previous night. He sat up in his chair and bounced the heels of his feet on the floor. Earl was usually a patient, easygoing man, but he was anxious to hear what Sandy had found out.

Normally, Sandy conducted the procedures himself with the help of his tech staff, but when there were multiple deceased persons or high-profile victims, he assigned coroners from other towns within the Floral County boundaries. For these autopsies, he borrowed a

husband-and-wife forensic team from Cottonfield, a town roughly the size of Floribunda about half an hour away.

Dr. Ken Le and Dr. Mai Le were third-generation American citizens descended from Asian immigrants. They had met and married while in medical school and moved to the small town in Florida after doing their residencies in the greater Atlanta area. They were known to be dedicated, meticulous, and highly intelligent, with an attention to detail that could have commanded them exorbitant salaries in a large metropolitan city, yet they preferred the slower, simpler life of Cottonfield's farming community.

Earl heard a series of dainty sneezes in the hallway.

"Bless you," he called.

"Thank you. Hello, Detective Petry." Mai Le smiled at him from the doorway. She rubbed her nose with a tissue. "I am allergic to cats. These men had cat fur on their clothing."

Earl stood up. "Hey, Dr. Le. Good to see you again. Thanks for coming in so early to help us out."

The petite young woman shrugged. "We're always up with the chickens ... literally. Ken greets them by name each morning. Truth be told, I think he secretly wants to be a farmer, but don't let him know I said so. We are nearly finished. Dr. Harper will be with you shortly. See you later." She trilled a high-pitched giggle and disappeared down the hall, juggling a tray of petri dishes and sample jars amid another series of sneezes.

Moments later, Sanderson Harper entered the

office and eased himself down into his battered leather desk chair. He was followed by a slender, black-haired man in his mid-thirties bearing two Styrofoam cups of coffee.

"Hello, Detective," Dr. Ken Le said. "How are things with you?"

"Not too bad, Ken. I just spoke to your bride. How are your chickens today?"

Dr. Le chuckled. "They're great. I found our first egg this morning. I think Eenie laid it."

Mai brushed in through the door and took a coffee from her husband, pulling out the scrunchie that held her sleek black hair in a ponytail. "Can you believe it? Ken named our chickens Eenie, Meenie, Miney, and Mo. Mo's a rooster."

"Love the names," Earl said with a grin. "What kind are they?"

"The three layers are Americaunas," Ken said. "Mai wanted them all to have traditional Vietnamese names, but I disagreed, since they are American chickens. We compromised on the rooster because he's a Chinese Silkie, and we call him Mo."

"Come, farmer Le. We have work to do in our own morgue," Mai said, "if Sandy's finished with us here."

"I think so. Can't tell you how much I appreciate your coming in on this one. I'll fill Earl in on the results," Sandy said. "You kids be safe. I'll let you know what we turn up as soon as I can."

Dr. Le ushered his wife out of the room, leaving

the two older men alone.

Earl shook his head. "I don't think I'd exactly call two thirty-five-year-old medical examiners 'kids,' if you know what I mean."

"Why not? They're the same age as my kids, but a whole lot smarter," Sandy said with a wry grin.

"That's true. Well, can you tell me what you and the 'kids' discovered?"

Sandy blew out a deep sigh, leaned forward, and spread out three manilla folders atop his desk. He opened the first folder and regarded his friend.

"Earl, what we have here are three adult men dead from cardiac events."

"So, heart attacks?"

"Yes ... and no. It's not that simple. Let me go through them one by one, and then we can discuss them."

"All right. Want to do them in order of death?"

"Sure. First victim. James Edgar Clay, known as Jimmy. Age 40. Height sixty-eight inches. Weight 170 pounds. Caucasian. Dyed black hair with grey roots throughout, worn short above the ears with front combed back Elvis-style. Dyed black goatee. Complexion olive, tanned. Eyes blue. No distinguishing marks except bilateral dimples in cheeks and an abdominal scar denoting a previous appendectomy. Facial contusions on right cheek consistent with being struck with an open hand."

"Witnesses said Jo Clay slapped him, and Santino Alvarez punched him in the face."

"Apparently. Deep bruising and lacerations on upper and lower lips. Mandibular fracture of the jaw consistent with a powerful blow from a closed fist." Sandy looked up at Earl. "He wore a partial upper dental plate consisting of front, incisor, and canine teeth. It was broken in half. And there was disruption of the cervical column, similar to a whiplash injury, along with blunt force trauma to the back of the head from hitting the road."

"Good Lord! That was a hell of a punch!"

"Ya think? He wouldn't have easily walked away from that fight."

"Did he die from the sucker punch?"

Sandy pursed his lips. "Certainly didn't help him. Now comes the interesting part. Actual cause of death was sudden cardiac arrest due to digoxin ingestion."

"Digoxin?"

"Uh huh, it's a drug commonly given to people with heart conditions. You probably know it as *Digitalis*."

"I've heard of it. Did he have some kind of preexisting heart condition?"

"Not that I could detect. He did suffer from ventricular tachycardia, according to his medical records."

"Which is ...?"

"Accelerated heart rate. He likely had an elevated blood pressure last night due to alcohol consumption."

"Yes. He was reportedly drunk."

"Blood alcohol was .20, so I can confirm that. It appears he ingested a large dose of *Digitalis* which triggered

the SCA."

"So, somebody gave him the *Digitalis,* or did he take it himself?"

"That's not likely, all things considered. You don't get a high from that kind of pharmaceutical. There's more. The SCA was complicated by the alcohol consumption, but he had also ingested a number of things which exacerbated the digoxin poisoning. Banana caused an excess of potassium, and black licorice caused an irregular heartbeat. Finally, hawthorn berry and Siberian ginseng dramatically increased the activity of digoxin in the body."

Earl paled. "Those sound like herbs, Sandy. Do you think ...?"

Sandy shook his head vigorously. "No way. Tommie didn't have any of those in her food, and she dispensed no herbal preparations at the event."

Earl relaxed. "There was a woman administering herbal potions. Padilla. Gertrudis Padilla."

"She's a local natural healer and herbalist in that community. Yeah. We took samples of her stock, but none of the herbs were in her preparations. Finbar Holmes served bananas, but they were definitely a food item that most of the crowd enjoyed with no ill effects."

"So, the key is the actual drug, compounded by the other things which he got somewhere."

"Correct. I have to rule his death as suspicious."

"Got it. Anything else?"

"There's a note here by Dr. Mai Le. She and Ken

did his autopsy. '*Suspect ingestion of Convallaria majalis and Digitalis purpurea.*' Lily of the valley and foxglove. That's interesting."

"Lily of the valley and foxglove? Did Mrs. Padilla have those in her booth?"

"No. We didn't find anything like that. No telling where he got 'em. I'll run another toxicology screen just to rule 'em out. We'll know more once we get results from the trace evidence."

"All right. That basically takes care of him for now. The next one is his brother."

Sandy opened the second folder. "Lawrence David Clay, known as Larry. Age 46. Height seventy inches. Weight 175 pounds. Caucasian. Medium brown hair with predominant gray at the temples. Worn in a short crew cut. Complexion olive. Slightly paler skin tone beneath a recently shaved full beard. Eyes blue. No distinguishing marks except bilateral dimples in cheeks and a Y-shaped groove on the mandible—what we call a chin dimple. Blunt force trauma to the nose and forehead from hitting the table face first. Rib fractures and internal bruising consistent with manual cardiopulmonary resuscitation, or CPR."

"Right. Dr. Frank performed CPR on Larry."

"Yes, but that had nothing to do with his death. He was DOA before the doctor did chest compressions. Again, I found evidence consistent with ventricular tachycardia, excess potassium from bananas, irregular heartbeat from black licorice, and increased digoxin in the

body from hawthorn berry and Siberian ginseng. He had ingested pharmaceutical *Digitalis*. He smelled like beer, but unlike his brother, there was no alcohol in his system."

"Who did his autopsy?"

"Ken Le. I don't find anything else in his notes, but we have to rule this death as suspicious, also. Once again, *Digitalis* is not a recreational drug. It has to be prescribed."

"Larry Clay was a pharmacist at the Rx-All—the head pharmacist, I believe."

"That's right, but there's no evidence of a preexisting heart condition. I can't think of any reason he'd have for taking *Digitalis*. Hmm. Here's a note from Mai. *"Suspect ingestion of Convallaria majalis and Digitalis purpurea."* Same thing as Jimmy Clay." Sandy frowned.

"What would lily of the valley and foxglove do to a person?"

Sandy regarded Earl and leaned backward in his chair. "They're both natural forms of digoxin. In fact, *Digitalis* is derived from the foxglove plant. Lily of the valley is a pretty, white flower, but it contains over 30 cardiac glycosides which can inhibit the heart's pumping activity. Consuming it would cause vomiting, diarrhea, and heart arrhythmia. I wonder ..." He opened the third folder and skimmed the contents. "Oh, dear Gussie. Here it is in Norman Frank's file. A note attached by Mai Le suspecting ingestion of foxglove plant and lily of the valley."

"Why didn't you find them, Sandy?"

"I did the gross and internal exams on the bodies

with Ken Le. Mai Le did all the tox panels and examination of stomach contents."

"What else did you find out about Dr. Frank?"

"His cause of death was exactly the same as Larry Clay's. Sudden cardiac arrest due to digoxin ingestion, with cardiac arrhythmia, excess potassium, irregular heartbeat, and increased digoxin activity in the body. Blunt force trauma to base of skull from hitting the street. Rib fractures and internal bruising from CPR. His was performed by Tommie. Same *Digitalis* poisoning, same ingestion of bananas, black licorice, hawthorn berries, and Siberian ginseng. The only difference is, according to Mai's note, he had ingested a concoction of hawthorn leaves and flowers, passionflower, peppermint leaf, basil leaf, parsley, celery juice, and olive oil. Those were the two herbal potions given to him by Mrs. Padilla when he began vomiting."

"Are those things deadly?"

"No. They're a harmless combination of natural ingredients."

"But you said hawthorn caused the body to create more digoxin."

"Hawthorn *berries*. The leaves and flowers are benign. It's the berries that ramp up the digoxin levels."

"Then, are you telling me that all three men died from heart attacks caused by the drug *Digitalis* and with poisonous herbs?"

"That's what I'm telling you."

Earl Petry planted his elbows on Sandy's desk and

laid his forehead in his upturned hands. "Oh, Lord. This is a nightmare! We've got a serial killer in Floral County."

"That's only part of your problem, Earl."

The men locked eyes and spoke simultaneously.

"Tommie."

Chapter Eight

TOMMIE WATSON savored the last bits of *Dublin Coddle Casserole* prepared and served by Finbar. When it was apparent her breakfast plate was scraped clean, Finbar took the dishes and set them in his sink to soak, poured two more cups of tea for Tommie and himself, and headed over to his favorite easy chair. Tommie had already taken her usual position on the adjacent sofa, her legs resting on a crocheted afghan atop the cushions. The three dogs sprawled on the floor.

Finbar propped his feet on a leather pouf and took a sip of the steaming brew before directing his gaze at his neighbor. "Are ye ready, missus?"

"Nine o'clock and all's well," Tommie quipped.

"So, it seems, Thomasina, except for the news ye got from yer cousin at the county morgue. What d'you make of his findings?"

"You were right, as usual. Definitely foul play."

Finbar took another sip of tea before reaching over to the side table and grabbing a stack of yellow legal pads. He laid them on his lap and regarded Tommie with a smile.

"Shall we begin, Watson? 'Tis a mystery we've to uncover—the cause of death to three healthy men amid a vast crowd of people, in front of the best detective team in Floribunda, Florida."

Tommie scoffed. "Yippee. The best sleuthing team around, and I haven't a clue what happened or how these men were poisoned in plain view."

"That's why we do this process, missus, to find the clues that will lead to the solution."

Finbar had devised the notepad method years earlier to help him solve televised mysteries, but Tommie had recently been instrumental in revising and honing the process. Together, they listed out the suspects, persons of interest, witnesses, motives, and facts on paper before taking to the streets and conducting in-person interviews. Thereafter, they compiled the salient information in their informal case files and brainstormed until they narrowed down the perpetrator or perpetrators, as the case may be.

"Finbar, I've got to tell you, I'm not really sure how to proceed. When Veranell died, we listed the people in the gazebo as suspects and the ones who presented prizes at the event as persons of interest. There were a lot of witnesses to interview. This time, we've got all the people who had food booths, as well as the ones having contact with the

victims. Plus, there's *three* victims! How do we even start?"

"Ach. I gave it some thought while I lay in m'bed last night." He held up the legal pads. "Elementary, dear Watson. Three victims. Three pads. We treat each of them as a different investigation. 'Twill be a bit of a stretch for us, but I've no doubt we'll prevail."

Tommie pushed herself up straighter against the back cushions. "That's brilliant. But you're right. It's going to be a lot more work. Might as well get started with the first to die. Jimmy Clay."

Finbar took the first pad and displayed what he had already written at the top in capital letters:

CRIME: DEATH AT CINCO DE MAYO FESTIVAL

Beneath that was written:

VICTIM I: JAMES "JIMMY" CLAY

WEAPON:

METHOD:

DATE/TIME: SUNDAY, MAY 5, 2019, 7:50 P.M.

DISCOVERED AT: MAIN STREET, GREENLEAF, FLORIDA (NEAR THE SOFT DRINK BOOTH)

DISCOVERED BY: CROWD AND VENDORS AT CINCO DE MAYO FESTIVAL

PRESENT:

Tommie whistled. "Wow, Finbar. You've been busy. OK. How do you want to itemize those present? Immediate vicinity?"

"Sure. I'm going to list Ms. Jo Clay, Santino Alvarez, and Leo Alvarez. We've already included the

crowd as a whole group."

"That works. Those were the people who were right there when he died. We'll make a note of any others as witnesses present when we get to that part of the list."

Finbar and Tommie worked together and filled in the next category, DESCRIPTION OF VICTIM, adding roughly the same information that Tommie's cousin had noted in his autopsy report.

"Can ye be more descriptive of his eye color, missus?" Finbar asked.

"Hmm. How about electric blue? They were very distinctive, and so were those dimples and that smile. His teeth were perfect and very white."

"Aye, but they were false."

"What? How do you know that?"

Finbar gave her an open-mouth smile. Without warning, he thrust his tongue forward and dislodged the six top front teeth, which were connected to a pink dental appliance by silvery wires.

Tommie yelped. "Ew, gross, Finbar!"

He laughed and pushed them back up in place with his thumb. "Got hit in the mouth with a hurling stick when I was in school. I takes them out at night and keeps them in a glass of water. They looks natural, don't ye think?"

"Uh, yeah. But how did you know Jimmy Clay wore a false plate?"

"When I served him, he tilted his head back to stuff the banana in, and I observed the little metal wires that

keeps the plate connected to the other teeth. It's all about being observant, Thomasina. Ye must be awares."

"Ew. If you say so. I was aware of his tight jeans and shirt unbuttoned to mid chest."

Finbar snorted. "Ye see what ye wants to see."

Tommie's face reddened. "He was easy on the eyes but not my type."

"As ye say, missus. As ye say. Let's go on."

OFFICIAL CAUSE OF DEATH (BY SANDERSON HARPER, FLORAL COUNTY CORONER)

Tommie nodded. "According to Sandy, the death is listed as suspicious. The cause was sudden cardiac arrest due to ... let me look at my notes ... oh, yeah ... *'digoxin ingestion from pharmaceutical Digitalis and complicated by alcohol, potassium, black licorice, hawthorn berry, and Siberian ginseng.'* So, I'd say a heart attacked induced by medication, alcohol, and herbs."

Finbar stopped writing.

"What?"

"I was just thinking about them herbs. D'you keep those in yer shop?"

"Black licorice and hawthorn leaves and flowers are non-toxic, but nobody I know has a need for the berries. They're deadly."

"Mrs. Padilla?"

"I can't believe she would have them either. I talked with the woman for a long time, and she showed me her preparations. If anything, she erred on the side of caution

with her tonics and used mostly food items. Do you think either one of us might be viewed as a suspect?"

"Ye know how people are, Thomasina. They mistrust what they don't understand, and herbal remedies are not viewed with the same regard as prescribed medications. I'm glad ye didn't give the man a tonic like ye did Mrs. Veranell Collins on Easter. At least we don't have to defend ye for that."

"I'll have to ask Gertrudis if she gave Jimmy Clay a potion at any time. What's next?"

Finbar consulted his list. "We'll fill in motive and weapon later. Let's do the suspect descriptions."

"OK. Who'd we say? Jo Clay, Santino Alvarez, and Leo Alvarez, right?"

"Aye. Let's begin with Ms. Clay."

"Finbar, because of Sandy's findings about the herbs, I think we should include Gertrudis Padilla as a suspect, even though we didn't see her with Jimmy Clay. What do you think?"

"I agree with ye, Thomasina. In fact, I'm going to leave a couple of blank pages in case we turn up someone else in our interviews." He wrote:

SUSPECT DESCRIPTIONS

I. GERTRUDIS PADILLA – HERBALIST

"I talked to her, so I'll describe her," Tommie said. "She's 58 years old. She stands a couple inches taller than me, so I'll say five foot four inches. Our weight is close. Maybe she's a little heavier. Let's put her about 210

pounds. She's Hispanic, from Mexico. She has a round build with very thick black hair and some grey throughout. She wears it all one length to her chin, pushed behind her ears, and tied with a colorful ribbon. She has dark brown eyes and wears black 'cheater' reading glasses held on a braided ribbon lanyard around her neck. Her skin is relatively smooth and medium tan. No makeup.

She's a widow with one child. Her daughter Lara lives in a mobile home next door to her and has an eight-year-old girl named Dearcilla. Gertrudis is an amateur herbalist who grows her own herbs and is teaching her granddaughter the craft. She attends *Iglesia de Santa Maria* in Greenleaf."

"Suspect two, Ms. Jo Clay."

2. JO(ANNE) CLAY – OWNER, THE CLAY PIGEON

"I'll do her, too," Tommie said. "Age 40. Five feet and five inches tall. Weight 145 pounds. Full-figured, dark green eyes, fair, freckled, Caucasian, long dark auburn hair worn pushed behind her ears. Divorced from Jimmy Clay. Engaged to Santino Alvarez. Will you do the brothers?"

Finbar wrote their names down and commented aloud as he filled in their descriptions.

3. SANTINO ALVAREZ – CO-OWNER, SANTINO'S SHOE SHOP, LEO'S LEATHER GOODS (W/BROTHER LEO).

"Santino is 40. He stands 5'8", 175 pounds. He is Mexican—a legal immigrant gaining citizenship. Muscular build, strong hands, brown skin tone, dark brown eyes, wavy black hair above the ears, handsome. He is a member

of the Church of Jesus Christ of Latter-day Saints, known as the Mormons. He speaks fluent Spanish and English and is engaged to Jo Clay."

4. LEO ALVAREZ – CO-OWNER SANTINO'S SHOE SHOP, LEO'S LEATHER GOODS (W/BROTHER SANTINO)

Finbar continued speaking and writing. "Leo is 38 and stands 5'8" tall, 155 pounds. He is also a legal Mexican immigrant gaining citizenship. He has a muscular build, brown skin, dark brown eyes, short straight black hair, and is a younger version of his handsome brother. He attends the same church, speaks fluent Spanish and English, and is engaged to Elly James of Elly's Jelly Jar."

"OK. I think that's all we can do for now on our first victim."

"Agreed. Well done, Thomasina. Let's take a break and refresh our tea before we venture on to the task of listing the persons of interest." He removed his reading glasses and laid the legal pads on the table.

"Good idea. I'm going to give Earl a call while you put the kettle back on, just to keep him in the loop."

Finbar snickered. "Keeping yer man in the loop will keep his woman out of the poop."

The cellphone in Tommie's pocket began to ring. "Ha, ha. Funny man, Finbar. How about you fix the tea, and I'll take this call."

Finbar busied himself in the kitchen while Tommie walked outside to talk on the phone. When she returned, her eyes were wide.

"Missus, what's happened?"

"Gertrudis Padilla has been detained at the station. They haven't formally charged her with all three deaths, but she's been marked as the prime suspect. That was her daughter, Lara. She's absolutely distraught."

"No! I can't believe it. What'd the lad say?"

"She begged for us to find out who did the killings and prove her mother innocent. Even offered us money."

"And did ye agree to help her mam?"

"Dang right, I did! For free, though. Bring the tea, Finbar. We've got three murders to solve ..."

"... and yer detective beau to consult with first."

Chapter Nine

EARL PETRY ended his call with Tommie and sat contemplating, with his fingers steepled in front of him as he sat at his desk.

"Hey, Earl. Has Ms. Watson begun her investigation yet?" Jenny asked, poking her head through the open door.

"Afraid so, Jenny. *'The game's afoot,'* as Finbar would say. They already know about Mrs. Padilla's pending arrest. I told Tommie the woman would be arraigned and likely released on her own recognizance if she's charged, and now Holmes and Watson will start asking their questions around town." Earl sighed deeply and rose to his feet.

"I know you worry, but they're surprisingly good at it, you know? And as long as she keeps you updated, we can really use their help … unofficially, of course."

Earl smiled wanly. "True. True. It's just that she always seems to attract trouble. How many times has she almost been killed because of her nosiness?"

"At least three times, to my knowledge. We'll be more vigilant about keeping her safe. Dale's got nights, and I have days. You have both." Jenny laughed brightly. "Meet you at the car. Oh, by the way, the fridge in the break room is loaded with leftovers from the festival. I took the liberty of writing our names on some of them."

"That was a great idea, Jenny. Those'll be the first ones eaten," he grumbled as he trailed along behind her.

When Earl turned the corner, he ran headlong into Dr. Norman Frank's French girlfriend Simone Lorence arguing with the desk sergeant.

"And who can tell me what has been found out about ze death of my fiancé?" she demanded, her arched brows raised. "You! Detective Petry! You were at ze festival when my darling Norman was killed. Do not tell me it was ze accident. I am sure he was murdered." She flicked her light blond, chin length hair back from her flashing green eyes and drew her full lips into an exaggerated pout as she positioned herself directly in front of the big man.

Earl took in her willowy 5'7" frame, manicured nails, and artfully made-up face and shifted his weight uneasily. Though she was probably no more than 130 pounds soaking wet, she had a commanding presence, but Earl had battled toe to toe with some adroit adversaries—including Tommie Watson—and he was not easily cowed.

"Miss Lorence. It's only 9:00 in the morning, and we've already been running down leads. I assure you, we're taking Dr. Frank's death very seriously."

"I do not zink you are at all. Shall I have Mr. Lassiter from my law office draft a legal document to be sure ze department *does* take zis death zeriously? Hmm?"

"That's certainly not necessary, but you go ahead and do what you have to do. We have processes in place, and right now, one of those processes is to interview witnesses. So, if you'll excuse me, you can leave your complaints with the desk sergeant while I try to find out who killed your boyfriend," he responded, sidestepping her and striding outside to the car.

"Earl?" Jenny said when he climbed in and slammed the door.

"Drive. I don't care where, just drive."

"Piece of work, isn't she?"

"Sure is. Did she accost you, too?"

"Me? Of course not. I'm just a lowly public servant and a woman at that. She was loaded for bear … and you're the bear. Better watch out. She'll be all over you like you don't know what."

"What's her story?"

Jenny shrugged. "From what I heard, she came here a few years ago from France by way of South Florida. Got a job as Harvey Lassiter's legal secretary. Harvey represented Dr. Frank in a malpractice case brought by Gertrudis and Lara Padilla over the wrongful death of

Salvador Padilla. Simone took a particular interest in the case and worked very closely with the doctor for the trial. He was acquitted without having to pay any settlement. Next thing you know, he's divorced Elaine Frank and moved Simone into his house. Ooh-la-la."

"Hmph. Drive through McDonald's and let me get a soda. I'll get you one, too."

"Ooh! That's a deal. Lights and sirens, partner?"

Earl chuckled. "Why not?"

Jenny bumped the siren once for good measure as she pulled onto Bottlebrush Boulevard. "Where to afterward?" she asked.

"Floribunda Real Properties. I think I'd like to have a chat with the sisters, Susan Clay and Elaine Frank, about their recently deceased ex-husbands!"

Chapter Ten

TOMMIE AND FINBAR continued their legal pad case files and filled in information for all three victims. The main suspects in Jimmy Clay's death were Gertrudis Padilla, Jo Clay, Santino Alvarez, and Leo Alvarez. Upon reflection, Finbar downgraded Leo to Person of Interest I.

"We can always change him back later, if we see the need, but I don't feel there's a strong case for himself to have a motive. D'you agree, missus?"

"Yes, I do. What about Lara Padilla? There was some contention between her and Jimmy Clay, and she was awfully protective of her daughter."

"I think we could make her suspect number four instead of Leo. Has she an occupation?"

"She's a checkout person at the Winn Dixie."

Finbar wrote her name on the pad.

4. LARA PADILLA – GROCERY CHECKER

"I'll describe her. She is early-to-mid-20s. She reminds me of myself at that age— petite, thin, and waiflike at 110 lbs. and just about my height of 5'2" or so. She's Hispanic and has shiny, layered black hair to her shoulders worn pushed behind her ears. Large dark brown doe eyes, medium tan complexion. I find her attractive, with a sweet smile and a quick laugh. It's obvious she's a good mother to her 8-year-old daughter Dearcilla. She must've had her while she was a young teenager. Gertrudis is Lara's mother."

"Righto. I'm looking at our other two victims, and the main suspects—besides Mrs. Padilla—would be their significant others who were tablemates—namely Mrs. Katherine Clay and Ms. Simone Lorence."

Finbar took the pad with Lawrence "Larry" Clay's name and copied the description of Gertrudis Padilla as Suspect I. He listed Larry Clay's wife as the fifth suspect.

5. KATHERINE CLAY – BOOKKEEPER

"Describe her, please, Thomasina."

"Katherine Clay. I remember her description from our last investigation. About 40, five feet nine inches, 150 lbs. She's Caucasian and has a fit build. She wears her honey blond hair in that trendy wavy chin bob. I think she has light brown eyes and a fair to medium complexion. She's attractive with a narrow nose, artful makeup, and manicured nails. She shops at Eva's Divas, Bettina's Baubles, Weller's Wine & Spirits, and upscale places like that. Larry is her second husband. She has two sons from her first

marriage. They're in middle school. She's a bookkeeper at Kitty Kare Kat Rescue and attends the First Baptist Church. She was one of the women in the mean girl club who doted on Veranell Collins."

"Is that right? She may bear a closer look. How about the other one—Simone Lorence?" He wrote her name on the legal pad.

6. SIMONE LORENCE – LEGAL SECRETARY

"She's also part of that group. From what I remember from our case notes, she's 35, five feet seven inches, 130 lbs., Caucasian. She's European—from France, I'm told—and looks it. She's got light amber-green eyes, an alabaster complexion, a curvy willowy build, large full lips, arched brows, manicured nails, artfully applied makeup. She wears her light blond hair in a squared-off bob to the chin with one side behind her ear—one of the few without that trendy wavy style.

Simone's a legal secretary at Lassiter Law Offices. She's single with no children. She lived with Dr. Norman Frank, Elaine's ex-husband. She attends the First Presbyterian Church—where Charles Williams went."

"And where yer cousin the coroner worships."

"Yup. Let's list Katherine as Suspect 2 and Simone as Suspect 3 on Dr. Frank's legal pad."

"Good on you, Thomasina. And, since Mrs. Padilla may be arrested, there must be some evidence against her, so I'll list her as Suspect 1 on all three victim charts. Now, until we go out and have conversations with

the townspeople, we won't know of any more suspects."

"I'm ready if you are, Finbar. Who's first?"

"Shall we begin at the beginning, missus? I say we motor off to Greenleaf and pay a visit to Mrs. Gertrudis Padilla and her daughter, Lara. We can get addresses of the local vendors from the two of them and then stop round at The Lunch Pad for a bite."

"Sounds like a plan. Maybe our chatty quartet will be able to meet us there for some juicy gossip."

"I do likes the way yer mind works, Dr. Watson. Let's crack on, shall we?"

Chapter Eleven

EARL PETRY sat comfortably in a padded barrel chair on wheels in the conference room at Floribunda Real Properties. Formerly called Floral Real Estate when it was owned and operated by Charles Williams and Beverly Cantrell, the business had undergone numerous changes since being acquired by Don Lareby, Elaine Frank, and Susan Clay.

Don still retained his job at First Floribunda Bank, but his sisters had quit theirs to run the real estate office. Their priority was to redo the décor. Their thinking was that people would be more inclined to part with a great deal of money if they felt at ease in their surroundings. Apparently, they were right, and the office was turning a tidy profit. Earl stood when the sisters entered.

"You're so polite, Detective. You needn't be that

formal with us," Susan said.

"For cripes sake, sister," Elaine quipped. "If the man wants to use good manners, let him."

The three of them sat down simultaneously and regarded each other with tentative smiles.

"Ahem. Nice to see you, ladies," Earl said.

"You, too, Earl. I know you're not here to buy a house, so let's get to the point," Elaine said.

"Sister! How about you use your own manners?" Susan turned to Earl with a smile. "What would you like to know? We're the gals with the information, after all."

Earl laughed aloud, nodding vigorously. "Manners or not, it's always refreshing to talk with you two. Well, you obviously know why I'm here. Yesterday's festivities gone wrong. What can you tell me about the events?"

Elaine leaned forward on her elbows at the conference table. "Right to the point, aren't you? Do you want to know about what we witnessed, or do you want the 'behind the scenes' version?"

Susan mirrored her sister's posture. "Or do you want to talk about our relationships with our recently departed ex-husbands?"

Earl matched their movements from across the table, pinpointing each one with his steel-grey eyes.

"I want you to tell me everything, ladies. Start with the actual events, then the unwitnessed scuttlebutt, and then we'll talk about your exes."

Both women leaned back in their chairs, grinning.

Earl listened as they provided their narrative in an alternating, tennis match style. He resisted the urge to turn his head from side to side.

"Wonderful," Susan said. "We got to our booth at 8:30 and began setting up our *Cinco de Mayo* food."

"We were Cabina 5. The tents were set up so that one side of the street was odd numbers, and the other side was even numbers," Elaine said.

"We were odd numbers."

"Obviously, if we were number five, sister."

"For cripes sake, sister. I'm just helping the man understand. You needn't be so rude."

"Sorry, sister. Anyway, we were the third booth on the left side of the street."

"I served *Salsa Roja Sedosa.* That was Jo's Silky Red Sauce."

"And I served *Salsa en Copas.* Elly's Jelly Jar Layered Sauce."

Earl interrupted. "Did you prepare the recipes?"

"Oh, no," Susan said. "Jo Clay made the red sauce and delivered it to my house."

"And Elly brought me her layered sauce in little quilted jelly jars."

"We just set, sold, and served them."

"We were doing well, too, until ..."

"... until Jimmy Clay came along and started causing trouble."

"Tell me about that," Earl said.

Elaine and Susan looked at each other and shrugged, then Elaine spoke up.

"Our booth was beside Lara Padilla's *pico de gallo* booth. It was right about 6:45. We had restocked from the lunchtime crowd. Jo had just left our booth and was getting some sauce at Lara's."

"Uh huh. Jo made these small, colorful bowls from clay in her shop specifically for that sauce, and she was holding a bowl in each hand when Jimmy accosted her."

"That's right. He put his hands all over her like he still owned her or something."

"They used to be married, you know, until she finally had the courage to leave his sorry self and get out of that cycle of abuse."

"He abused her?" Earl asked.

"Oh, yes," Susan said. "He ran around on her something terrible. Just like Larry ran around on me."

"But Larry never hit you, sister, or made you do unspeakable things in the bedroom," Elaine said.

Susan's face colored. "That's true. But back to the point. Jimmy was groping Jo right out there in public, and she was pretty upset."

"Where was her fiancé? Where was Santino Alvarez when all this was happening?" Earl asked.

"I think he was at another booth across the way … maybe Tommie's. I'm not sure," Elaine said.

"Anyway, Lara's little daughter was helping her in the booth by handing out the sauce. She had just served Jo

and was standing right beside her when Jimmy knocked Jo's hand against the table and made her break the bowl."

"Dearci began to cry because she had helped make all the bowls in Jo's ceramics shop."

"And then that jerk grabbed Jo's hand holding the broken bowl and drank the sauce out of it. He licked it all over ... even her hand! It was disgusting!"

"Crap on a cracker! I thought I'd lose my lunch."

Earl grimaced at her comment. "And ...?"

"And then he looked over at Lara and leered at her." Susan demonstrated her version of a leer, narrowing her eyes and raising her eyebrows up and down.

Earl blinked rapidly. "Uh, I see. When did the face slap occur?"

"Oh! That was right afterward when Jimmy turned his attention to Dearci."

"Cute little girl. Too bad her worthless father showed up." Susan clapped her hand over her mouth.

"Whoa, whoa, whoa. Who's her worthless father?" Earl sat up in his chair.

"Um, er ... Jimmy Clay. Isn't that who we were just talking about?" Susan stammered.

"Jimmy Clay was Dearci's father?"

Elaine's eyes widened. "Well, of course. All you needed to do was look at her to know that. Little Hispanic child with blue eyes and dimples. Spitting image of him."

"That's right. And he knew it. That's why he touched her. He put his hand under her chin and made her

look at him. Then he said, 'I know where you got them eyes, girl.' I thought Lara would come unglued."

"She *did* come unglued. She snatched that little girl back behind the counter before he could say any more."

"Then Jimmy laughed real loud and smacked Jo on the bottom."

"And she yelped and clobbered him good! It was the slap heard around the world."

"But he didn't even flinch. He just kept laughing."

"That's when Santino made his appearance ... after he heard that slap and Jo's shout."

"Is that when Santino punched him?" Earl asked.

"Nah ah. That was later. Jo got between them and moved Santino away, but not before Santino said, 'you ever touch her again, I'll kill you.' I don't think he really meant he'd kill him, Earl. He was just mad, you know?" Susan's eyes were wide.

Elaine was equally wide-eyed. "The punch came about an hour later when Jo went to the soft drink tent. Jimmy came up behind her and threw his arms around her."

"He was drunk as a skunk. He'd been sitting at the table with Larry, Katherine, Simone, and Norman. I saw him chug at least three beers."

"Leo and Santino were at Cabina 6, right across from us. Donny and Henry were at that booth selling corn on a stick and the beef jerky the Alvarez brothers had made. Jo and Elly went to get drinks. Jimmy saw them walk away from the brothers, and that's when he followed them."

"And in just a couple of minutes, Santino noticed him and took off with Leo right behind."

The two sisters leaned forward toward Earl with their hands flat on the conference table.

"Jo screamed," Elaine said.

"Santino grabbed Jimmy and swung him around," Susan said.

"Santino drew back and punched him in the jaw."

"Jimmy was knocked off his feet and landed on his back on the street."

"Leo pulled Santino away. Jo ran to his side, and Elly ran to Leo's."

Susan's eyes filled with tears. "Larry stood up from the table and looked their way. Then, he just collapsed."

Elaine reached over and patted her sister's hand.

"Norman got down and hovered over him, trying to do CPR. But he started heaving and vomiting," she said.

Both women were sniffling and holding hands.

"What happened next, ladies?" Earl asked.

Susan wiped her eyes. "Gertrudis Padilla came weaving through the crowd holding two small glass bottles. She helped Norman into his chair and had him drink whatever was in the bottles."

Elaine sniffed. "He looked like he was a little better, but all of a sudden, he jerked backwards and fell to the ground. Then Tommie rushed over from across the street and started pumping on his chest, but it was no good. He was dead. Our poor husbands, Larry and Norman, were

both dead."

The women cried in earnest, dabbed at their eyes, and blew their noses with frilly handkerchiefs produced from who-knows-where. Earl, at a complete loss for words, sat and watched them in silence.

A soft knock at the open door drew their attention.

"Earl," Jenny Foran said, "Sorry to interrupt, but we need to get back to the station."

Earl rose to his feet. "All right, Jenny. Ladies, thank you for your help. My condolences for your losses."

Elaine and Susan beamed at him through their tears and waved their handkerchiefs as he exited the door.

"What's up at the station, Jenny?" Earl asked as he climbed in the car.

Jenny snickered. "Nothing. I came inside to use the restroom and heard the waterworks. I thought you might need rescuing. Always got your back, partner."

"Just for that, I'll buy your lunch. Back to McDonald's, partner."

Chapter Twelve

TOMMIE AND FINBAR pulled up to Gertrudis Padilla's home at roughly the same time Earl was wondering how to deal with the weeping sisters. From the street, the house had a definite, if modest, curb appeal, with its white clapboard siding and grey shingled roof. A low picket fence encased the front yard, with a little gate opening onto a bricked walkway flanked by tidy rows of various herbs.

Two wooden window boxes painted a bright rose color held marigolds, petunias, and dandelions on the right side of the house, while two identical window boxes on the left side held what Tommie recognized as basil, flat and curly parsley, and three kinds of mint. A huge pot beside the front door overflowed with rosemary. The smell wafted toward Tommie as she exited the car, and she smiled. It was, without a doubt, an herbalist's home.

Finbar had called ahead, and Gertrudis Padilla met them at the door. She was a sturdy woman, and she greeted them with a weary, but genuine smile.

"*Buenos días.* Welcome to my home. Please, come inside. I am so happy you're here to visit."

"Halloo, madame," Finbar said. "We've come to see if we can right yer unfortunate situation. Yer lovely daughter asked us to help." He made his way to the floral armchair she offered.

Lara waved at them from inside the living room where she sat in a matching slipper chair. "Thank you so much, Mr. Holmes, Ms. Watson."

Tommie took a seat on the cushioned sofa. "Please, call us Finbar and Tommie. We're here as your friends."

"May I offer you some tea?" Gertrudis asked. "It is my own herbal blend."

"Lovely," Finbar said. "Thomasina will take hers with a sweetener, but I've the diabetes, so plain for me."

Gertrudis disappeared into the kitchen, and Tommie took the opportunity to speak to Lara.

"Is your mother all right after the interrogation at the police station? She looks worn."

"She's upset and embarrassed. Nothing like this has ever happened to her. She's afraid for her reputation as a healer and herbal practitioner. And, of course, it will be so hard to pay out money for her bail if she's charged."

"I certainly understand her feeling. I've been a suspect several times, but I've not been formally arrested. It

must be awful to have that looming over you."

"More than you can imagine. I only hope you and Mr. Holmes ... Finbar ... can prove her innocence."

"We shall do our best, lad," Finbar said. "D'you know what evidence the police have on yer mam?"

"I don't know for sure, but Mama will tell you. Let me go help her with the tea."

Lara jumped up from her chair and met her mother at the doorway. Taking the wooden tray from Gertrudis, she set about pouring steaming tea into colorful oversized ceramic mugs.

Tommie breathed in the fragrant herbal blend. "Mmmm. Chocolate mint, licorice root, and ginger. What a great combination."

"You have a good nose," Gertrudis said.

"Thank you." Tommie added agave syrup into her mug and examined the tiny decorations on the surface. "I thought at first these were painted, but the flowers are pressed into the clay. Did you make these, Gertrudis?"

"Oh no. They are made by my granddaughter, Dearcilla. She is quite taken with ceramics. She loves to go to Miss Jo's shop every chance she gets."

"Well, she's got a knack for sure. I recognize chamomile flowers, mint leaves, honeysuckle blossoms. Oh, and look ... pine nuts, too. How clever!"

"Thank you." The soft soprano voice came from behind Lara's chair.

"Dearci, come on out," her mother said.

The little girl peeked her head around the chair. She was barely four feet tall and maybe 50 pounds soaking wet. She gazed at them from behind large blue eyes ringed with thick dark lashes. Her long black hair was pulled into a high ponytail and caught with a purple scrunchie holder which matched her lavender unicorn t-shirt. She smiled shyly, displaying deep dimples in her cheeks and a matching dimple in her chin.

"You are an artist, Dearci," Tommie said. "If I had beautiful mugs like this in my shop, I would sell lots and lots of tea."

Dearci giggled, then she regarded Tommie solemnly. "I can make you some. Miss Jo lets me make lots of things. If you help my *abuela,* I will make you some."

Tommie swallowed and struggled to keep her eyes from misting. "I will help your grandmother, Dearci. I promise I will help her."

Dearci's eyes brightened, and she ran to her grandmother and whispered in her ear. When Gertrudis nodded, Dearci skipped to the kitchen and returned holding two tiny bowls out for the guests. Tommie recognized them as identical to the same ones used to hold the salsa the previous day.

"Miss Tommie. This one is for you to keep. And this one is for you, Mr. Holmes."

"Ah, thank you, lad. 'Tis most kind of you," Finbar said with a wink.

Dearci giggled. "*Abuela,* may I go to the garden to

look for good flowers for Miss Tommie's mugs?"

Gertrudis nodded. "*Sí, Chiquita.* But do not pick any yet or your flowers will wilt. Wait until you are ready to go to the Clay Pigeon."

"Why don't you get your sketch book and draw the flowers you want to use?" Lara suggested.

Dearci beamed and ran to her playroom. The slam of the back door let them know she was out of earshot.

"Good on you for that suggestion, lad. 'Tis better she is not around to hear us discuss murder and things unseemly for innocent children," Holmes said.

The time passed quickly as the adults talked. Gertrudis painstakingly took them through the ingredients and processes she used in the preparations she had on hand in her booth at the *Cinco de Mayo* celebration while Finbar took copious notes.

"How did ye know what potion to give Dr. Frank when he began to vomit?" he asked. "How did ye diagnose his ailment?"

Gertrudis flicked her eyes to her daughter before answering. "I knew the signs. My husband, Salvador, had a heart condition. Dr. Frank was his cardiologist. He took a medicine prescribed by Dr. Frank. Many times, it made him sick, and many times I had to give Salvador a potion to ease his discomfort. That is the potion I gave to Dr. Frank. I also take a potion for my own congestive heart failure. I would not take a medicine from Dr. Frank."

Something in her tone of voice alerted Tommie.

"What exactly did Dr. Frank prescribe for your husband?"

"*Digitalis.* It did not agree well with him."

"What did you give him to counteract his adverse reaction to it?"

"I treated him with a tincture of peppermint leaf, basil leaf, and parsley, and when the sickness was very bad, I gave him a dose of celery juice and olive oil."

"Are those what you gave Dr. Frank?"

"The very same, yes."

"Did you, by chance, add anything else? Black licorice, hawthorn berries, Siberian ginseng?"

Gertrudis looked startled. "No. I wouldn't use that combination of herbs. Without a patient history, I wouldn't know what type of interactions it would cause."

"In yer professional opinion, how would a person happen to consume them?" Finbar asked.

"Black licorice is a food herb. It is common enough in sauces and candies, like the *tamarindos* that Padre Sanchez gave the children or as a syrup for coughing and in the tea you are drinking. Siberian ginseng is a specialty herb we call *Diablo's arbusto.* Devil's shrub. Mostly, men ask for it to help them make their wives happy in the bedroom. It is never used for people with heart conditions."

"And hawthorn berries? I know the leaves and flowers are used for heart preparations, but the berries are too potent. I don't stock them," Tommie said.

Gertrudis reached into her apron pocket and removed a small glass vial. "I use them, but only for myself.

Hops, cayenne pepper, hawthorn berries, and black licorice root in very specific proportions with apple juice, honey, ginger, and cinnamon. This syrup is my own personal recipe. I do not give it to anyone else."

Tommie locked eyes with Gertrudis. "All three men had traces of black licorice, hawthorn berries, and Siberian ginseng in their system, as well as the pharmaceutical *Digitalis*. They also had ingested lily of the valley flowers and foxglove. Do you grow those?"

Gertrudis Padilla turned pale and crossed herself rapidly. "*Dios mio,*" she whispered. "I do have a few foxglove plants in my garden, but the flowers are only to be used with great care. They are dangerous. I once added a pinch of lily of the valley leaf in my heart potion, but it gave me a bad reaction, so I pulled the plants up and burned them in a pit in the woods behind my house. How those men got them, I do not know. A thing like that I could never do. I cannot use my plants to kill a person. Never." She made the sign of the cross again.

Finbar cleared his throat. "Mrs. Padilla. Ye must excuse me, but I has to ask. Did ye have any ill feelings against any of the dead men?"

Gertrudis and Lara exchanged another look.

"I can answer that," Lara said. "You better believe it. We both had ill feelings against all three of those men."

"Lara, *por favor,*" her mother said.

"No, Mama. They are here to help. They need to know everything. Oh yes. There were problems. The good,

upstanding Dr. Frank? That's a laugh. He killed my father."

"What?" Tommie's jaw dropped open.

"You heard my mother tell you that the medicine Dr. Frank gave him made him sick. That is true. But what she didn't say was that it caused him to have heart failure, and when we got him to the Urgent Care for help, Dr. Frank only prescribed more of the medicine in a bigger dose. We asked the pharmacist if it was too much medicine, but he said Dr. Frank was a good doctor who knew what he was doing, and he wouldn't change the prescription. A week later, my father died in his bed."

"What did ye do, lad?" Finbar asked.

"There was an autopsy done before we could bury my father. The coroner said it was too much digoxin in his system. We tried to sue Dr. Frank, but he had a better lawyer who threw all kinds of legal and medical terms around that impressed the judge and the jury. They acquitted the so-called 'doctor' without even a settlement for wrongful death."

"And the chemist? What of him?"

"You mean the pharmacist? He wasn't even implicated or charged with negligence. In fact, he was promoted to the head pharmacist of the Rx-All."

"And yer man's name was ...?"

"Larry Clay." Hearing the back door slam, Lara jumped up and headed Dearci off. The two of them disappeared into the little girl's playroom.

"So, Dr. Frank and Larry Clay were responsible for

your husband's death." Tommie said. "I'm so sorry, Gertrudis. I'm sure it's been hard on your family."

"*Sí*. I have tried not to hold any hatred in my heart for these men, but Lara has yet to forgive them."

"I saw Lara arguing with Jimmy Clay when he was at her booth yesterday. I believe he was bothering Dearci."

Gertrudis scowled. "Jimmy Clay had no good qualities whatsoever. He stalked my daughter and constantly harassed her. How dare he lay a hand on my granddaughter, too!" She glanced back toward the hallway where Lara and Dearci went. "Those men did much damage to my family. Much damage." She pressed her lips together and shook her head. "They left us without husband, father, and grandfather. And the worst part. That Clay man forced his way on my Lara when she was only 16 years old."

Chapter Thirteen

TOMMIE punched a button on her phone and slipped it back into her side pocket.

"Apparently, Earl interrogated Elaine and Susan and got them all upset, so they're not going to meet us today. It's early, yet, but I have to be at the shop by noon to open up. Still want to go to The Lunch Pad?" she asked.

"Sure, sure. 'Tis nearly time to eat, and I've nothing to prepare for us. We can dine with the gossipy quartet another day," Finbar said.

Tommie parked behind the space-themed diner, and the two of them entered through the back door. A trio of voices sang out to them in three-part harmony before they even made it into the dining room.

"Tommie! Finbar! Over here!" The summons came from Tommie's musical Community College Chorus friends—Joan Carroll, Tina Brass, and Annie Lang.

Finbar shrugged and followed Tommie to the table

where the boisterous women sat. He smiled graciously.

"Halloo, songbirds. 'Tis a pleasure to see ye once again. Might we join ye?"

The women giggled and nodded, hugging Tommie and rearranging themselves so all five could fit around the circular table.

They were about as dissimilar as three ladies could possibly be. Joan, who was of sturdy Nordic descent, was 62 and stood nearly six feet tall. She had light blue eyes, a medium complexion, and wore her wavy dark blond hair in a chin length style with bangs. Tina was 73, several inches shorter and many pounds lighter, pale, with azure blue eyes and soft grey hair cut above her ears. Annie was barely five feet tall and pudgy, with a crown of russet curls, olive skin, and squinty dark brown eyes that shone from behind cat-eye reading glasses. They were, respectively, single, widowed, and divorced.

The "Songbirds" (as Holmes liked to call them) had forged a fast friendship with Tommie as soon as they heard her sing when she joined the chorus at the local community college. Upon their first meeting with Finbar, they had adopted him, as well. Though they didn't have the gossip news Tommie and Finbar liked to access from the Fab Four, theirs was another indispensable network of information that ran even deeper: as local born and bred residents, they were related to most of Floral County.

"Are you hot on the hunt?" Joan asked. The last word ended in a swooping upward inflection.

"What hunt would that be?" Tommie played coy.

"The triple deaths, of course. Finding the killer," Tina said. The word took an up and down musical turn.

Tommie batted her lashes. "Mmm. We're doing a little checking around."

Annie punched Joan on the shoulder. "Told you they weren't natural deaths. If they were, Holmes and Watson wouldn't be on the case. Besides, I heard they might arrest *Señora* Padilla for three murders." The pitches of the words progressed from low to high and back to low.

"Yes, in fact, we've just come from there, Tommie leaned in closer to her friends, "but we don't really think she did it."

"Is that a fact?" Joan said. "Give us details!"

Finbar was amused at the musicality with which they spoke. Every sentence seemed to end with a tonal interval in a rhythmic cadence in a distinctive pattern: one-syllable words became two-syllable words and were stressed on the first syllable; three-syllable words (or two combined words) were spoken with the middle syllable emphasized.

"Have ye ordered, lads? M'self, I'm right perishing from hunger."

"We've just done that, Mr. Holmes. You and Tommie can share with us. We always order the *Solar System Sub Sandwich Sampler.* There's plenty for leftovers or for a crowd. You will *adore it!*" Tina trilled.

The decision having been made for him, Finbar sighed, closed the menu, and sat back in his chair, content to sip on his ice water and let Tommie carry out the investigative conversation with her harmonizing friends.

"So, can you tell us anything substantial?" Joan

asked. "Can *we* tell *you* anything substantial?"

"Yes, you can. For starters, what do you know about Larry and Jimmy Clay?" Tommie asked.

Joan and Annie swiveled their heads toward Tina.

"Grandma was married to a Clay. A great uncle to those two boys. All the men in that family had a 'runaround gene' that was pretty strong. And they usually went after the young attractive ones. Larry and Jimmy were my second cousins once removed," she said.

"As I recall, there was another gene that was pretty strong in them. The dimple gene," Joan said.

"So true. It kept popping up like a bad penny. That and the blue eyes. I got the eyes, but not the dimples. But, if you look around town, you'll see lots of identical eyes and dimples." Tina opened her own eyes wide.

Annie snickered. "Like the Padilla grandchild. The little girl got the *chin* one, and that was less common."

Tina scowled. "All right. That's enough of that. It's beginning to sound like gossip, and that's unseemly."

Tommie quickly changed the subject. "Are any of you related to Dr. Frank or his girlfriend, Simone?"

The three ladies shook their heads.

Joan shrugged. "They're both transplants. No relatives in town except for Elaine Frank, who was married to the doctor. She and Don and Susan are cousins on my father's side of the family."

"Then that so-called French woman came along and stole the doctor away with her accent," Annie said.

"And the other charms I don't think I should mention," Tina said with a toss of her head. "Cousin Larry was married to Elaine's sister, Susan. They didn't have any children, but I know Larry wanted to be a father. Katherine Howell came along, and she was younger and had two boys. One was in kindergarten, and one was in preschool. She told Larry she was pregnant, and he divorced Susan to marry her. Then she claimed she lost the baby and had to get a hysterectomy. That ended his chances of carrying on the legitimate Clay line and last name."

"Legitimate being the key word," Annie said.

Tommie gasped. "You mean ...?"

Annie nodded her head. "You can spot his and Jimmy's offspring around town, but none of them have the Clay last name ... just the azure blue eyes and dimples. Katherine ... she's a third cousin on my mother's side from Greenleaf ... she wanted Larry to formally adopt her two boys, but he wouldn't. Men can be funny about paternity."

Just when Finbar thought he might have to leave the table to give his ears a rest, the food arrived.

The spread was, indeed, plenty for a crowd. It was served on a huge round lazy Susan within arm's reach of all the diners at the table. Finbar's eyes widened as the waitress filled the board with *Black Hole Brioche Buns*, deli sliced *Cosmic Cold Cuts*, a *Man in the Moon Cheese Plate* (thankfully, no green cheese), *Astronaut Add-ons* (sliced tomatoes and onions, pickle relish and spears, and shredded lettuce), an array of condiments, including *Moon Landing*

Mayonnaise, yellow and brown *Meteor Mustard,* and *Orbit Oil and Venus Vinegar,* and two large bowls which held *Pluto Potato Salad* and *Comet Coleslaw.* Foregoing any notion of "ladies first," he assembled a gigantic sandwich in record time. Nobody noticed his lack of manners; they were all doing likewise.

"Annie," Tommie said through a mouthful of sandwich. "Why did you say Simone was 'so-called' French? She wasn't?"

Annie took a swallow of water. "She said she was a descendant of Charles de Lorencez, the Frenchman who lost the *Battle of Puebla* that was celebrated yesterday. For the past few years, she's gotten up and given a speech in the name of her great-great-grandfather declaring victory to the Mexicans to ingratiate herself with the Latina community."

"And she isn't a descendant?"

"No way! I traced that line back from the 1800s. Supposedly, according to Simone, Charles Ferdinand Latrille de Lorencez had a daughter named Emilia Perez de Lorencez, who had a son named Charles Luis Lorence, who fathered Ferdinance Lorence, who was Simone's father. It simply didn't happen. Charles de Lorencez's line ended with Emilia in the early 1900s."

Tommie stared open-mouthed at her friend. "How do you *know* all that?"

Annie giggled. "I've been compiling my genealogy at the LDS church where Joan and Tina attend."

"We all meet there on Tuesdays to work on our

family trees, don't we ladies?" Tina said to the nods of the other two.

"OK. But what made you research her line, Annie?"

"My ancestor is Rafaela Zaragoza nee Padilla. He was the grandfather of Ignacio Zaragoza nee Padilla who *won* the *Battle of Puebla* that was celebrated yesterday."

"Did you say 'Padilla' was his name?"

"Oh yeah. Didn't I tell you already? I'm of Mexican heritage. Many of my relatives live in Greenleaf. Gertrudis Padilla is my cousin."

Chapter Fourteen

EARL brought Jenny back to the station to grab some lunch before her shift with Dale. He heard her grumble when she checked the refrigerator. Sure enough, the *Cinco de Mayo* containers with their names on them were emptied and in the trash. She threw her hands in the air, grabbed Dale, and the two of them left for fast food.

Earl pawed through the remaining leftovers, came up with enough to make a decent meal, and wolfed it down after a quick nuke in the microwave. Checking his watch, he drove his own car to town to have a conversation with the Alvarez brothers. He found them in a heated argument when he entered the back door of their shop.

"*Hermano,* I told you to take care. That man was not worth the attention with a fight. We may be in serious trouble now," Leo said.

Santino paced in a tight circle. "*Comprendo,* Leo. I understand. But I could not stand by when he molests my fiancé. I did not hit him so hard."

"Santino, you broke his jaw. I heard it. Do not forget what happened last time you broke a man's jaw."

Earl stepped into the store. "What happened last time you broke a man's jaw, Santino?"

The brothers whirled around to face the big detective. Their eyes were wide.

"*El señor detective,*" Santino said. "We did not hear you come in. *¿Que pasa?* Is all well with you?"

"Peachy. But all is not well with you, apparently."

"No, no. I feel badly about that man who died. Did I kill him, Earl? I did not think I hit him so hard."

"Everybody said it was a pretty solid punch, and it appears you were protecting Jo. But what makes you think you killed him?"

Santino frowned and cleared his throat. "My brother said he heard the jaw crack, and the man landed on the street and hit his head very hard. I am very afraid I hurt him too badly. I did not mean to use so much strength."

Leo nodded. "*Sí, sí.* It is true, *señor.* I was right there. He only hit one time, right on the chin. I think the man stumbled and fell. That may be how the jaw broke."

"Maybe. Maybe not. Regardless, you were within your rights to use force to get him off of Jo. Not *deadly* force, mind you, but force nonetheless," Earl said.

"I did not intend to be deadly. I only meant to get

his filthy hands off my fiancé. He had assaulted her once already that afternoon. I did not punch him that time ... but I wanted to. He deserved it."

"But you did not hit him, *hermano*." Leo pressed his lips together tightly and lifted his head. "I would have done the same thing if that man had touched my Elly. And he was *muy borracho*. Very drunk."

"That's what I've been told," Earl agreed. "Do either of you know why he targeted Jo?"

"*Sí*, Earl. My Jo was once married to Jimmy Clay. She told me of the terrible things he would do to her. He struck her often, and he forced her as a husband should never force a wife. There was no love in the marriage from him. Only control and pain. And to make it worse, he had relations with other women ..."

"No, Santino. Not just other women. Elly said it was also other *girls*. Young ones who were innocent and afraid of him." Leo shifted his weight from foot to foot. "He even tried to be with Elly, but she fought him off. She told me Jimmy Clay had raped a girl who was in high school and made her pregnant."

Earl blanched. "Did she say who the girl was?"

Leo and Santino exchanged a guarded look. "*Señor*, I am sorry to tell you, but the girl was Lara Padilla. Her *chiquita*, Dearci, is the baby he fathered," Leo said.

"Did she ever report the attack?" Earl asked.

"Jo told me the girl had been given a bad reputation. It may have been Jimmy Clay who passed the

rumor around. But there was talk that she had been intimate with other adult men about the same time. Jo said Lara thought nobody would believe her," Santino said.

"That does happen, I'm sad to say. But if the girl was promiscuous with other men, how can Jo be sure Jimmy Clay fathered Lara's child?"

"Oh, you must see the resemblance in the *hija pequeña*. The little girl has the blue eyes and the dimples. They are hard to mistake."

"And there's another thing that is a giveaway," Leo said. "The *chica's* name."

"What about her name?" Earl asked.

Santino raised his head to meet Earl's eyes. "They call her Dearci, but that is a short name . . . a nickname. Her full name is Dearcilla."

Leo stepped up beside his brother. "In Spanish, it would be written *de arcilla*. That means 'of clay.' Lara Padilla herself tells the child's parentage."

Chapter Fifteen

TOMMIE was unusually busy for a Monday in Watson's Reme-Teas, dispensing steaming mugs of her latest herbal blends—*Minty May Day Matcha* and *Lemon-Lime Llama Tea.* Her customers buzzed excitedly as they ate their brown bag lunches at the seven round tables set up in her shop. She had recently added a new sweetener, and her patrons seemed to enjoy the vanilla bean-infused powdered stevia she called *Stevanilla.*

The theme for May centered around *Is Your Mama a Llama?*—a popular book written by Deborah Guarino and illustrated by Steven Kellogg. A former elementary school teacher, Tommie selected a different book each month on which to base her display window decorations and specialty tea blends. In honor of *Cinco de Mayo,* Mother's Day, and of her friends' engagements,

she decided to bring in a distinct Hispanic theme as well.

Though Tommie was usually closed on Saturdays, her free-spirited new-age Riverton friend Maggie Kohl had suggested she host a story time event to drum up more revenue for the shop.

"But Maggs, I have plenty of business during the week," she had complained.

"I know, Tommie, but I saw it in the cards. You must engage the little children and their mothers in hearing you read the stories. You read aloud to all the students at school, and the parents fought tooth and toenail to have their kids enrolled in your class. I drew the nine of Pentacles paired with The Empress for you. You are the woman in the garden holding a bird on her hand surrounded by coins, and you will sit on the throne in a flowing robe, full of feminine energy, creative power, and abundance. You will blossom and reap the fruits of your labors so you can enjoy the finer things life has to offer. I have seen it!" Maggie's blue eyes glistened beneath her flowing cascade of platinum waves and curls.

"All right. If you're so sure, I guess I can add a Saturday morning event to read from whatever book I use to decorate the store each month."

Maggie clapped her hands. "It will be so, Tommie. I will come to your first reading in May, and I'll bring Terry Jackson. We are your biggest fans."

"Thanks, Maggs. Only, instead of me reading this first month, I think I'll have my friends Leo and

Santino Alvarez read the book in Spanish while their fiancés Elly James and Jo Clay read in English. It can be a multicultural event."

"Brilliant idea! And don't worry about making food. It's a story time, not a luncheon. You just focus on the decorations and your guest readers. Many blessings, Tommie, until then."

Maggie's cards seemed to be right. The event the previous Saturday had been well attended. Adults filled the chairs while the children lounged on individual carpet squares laid on Tommie's floor. Jo started the story off by reading a page, followed by Santino translating the page in Spanish. Then Elly read a page with Leo providing translation. Afterwards, Tommie mingled with the adults while the children clamored over the four guest readers, looking at the storybook pictures and trying out the Spanish words.

Two days later, and Tommie had noticed a decided increase in her business all afternoon. While she worked, she sipped on a concoction of peppermint leaves and flowers, dill leaves and seeds, and raw tupelo honey. *The Rumbly Tummy Reme-Tea* was just what she needed after overindulging and wolfing her food down at The Lunch Pad with the Songbirds earlier.

Finbar went next door to his own shop, Caife Caife Holmes, and prepared for his evening coffee rush. Tommie would join him at 5:00 after she closed her shop to help him serve Irish coffee and snacks to his customers. At the

moment, however, she was preoccupied with the menu and the recipes for next Sunday's Mother's Day Tea Party. May 12 was also Tommie's 65th birthday, but she had no plans to celebrate it or incorporate it into her Sunday event.

She decided to introduce two new beverages for the tea party. She got busy chopping the dehydrated cranberries that would be added to the Red Rooibos tea with hibiscus flowers and red rose petals. When she finished, she mixed the ingredients together and placed them in two gallon-sized zipper bags. She would add a generous tablespoon of fresh pomegranate seeds to each steeping mug of *Té de Flores Rosado* (Rosy Flowers Tea) prior to serving.

The second beverage was *Chocolate Caliente con Hielo* (Hot Chocolate on Ice). Tommie mixed ground cinnamon, vanilla extract, orange zest, and maple syrup with finely chopped raw coca nibs, carob, and dark chocolate. She spooned the paste into a large zipper lock bag and placed it in the undercounter refrigerator. On Saturday, she would add the mixture to almond milk and carefully melt it in a large pot atop her induction cooktop. The creamy blend would be served over ice cubes in mugs.

The lunch menu itself would be a variety of finger sandwiches which would correspond to the characters in the book: bats, swans, cows, seals, kangaroos, and llamas. She planned to prepare six types of "mother" sandwiches and six types of "child" sandwiches. Finbar had agreed to help with the preparation during the week.

Tommie checked her growing list of ingredients:

chicken breasts, smoked salmon, tuna, pepperoni slices, deli-style ham, eggs, two types of sliced cheese, cream cheese, sun dried tomatoes, avocados, garbanzo beans, green and black olives, pimentos, garlic, bananas, grapes, limes, lemons, raisins, dill and sweet pickle relish, mayonnaise, mustard, yogurt, sour cream, parsley, cumin, olive oil, peanut butter, hazelnut spread, agave syrup, and marshmallow fluff. She also added 12 types of breads: potato, French, white, raisin, challah, multigrain, ciabatta, pretzel, brioche, baguettes, pita pockets, and Hawaiian-style sweet rolls.

Tommie grimaced and pulled out her phone to check her bank balance. *Phew!* She blew out her breath in a sigh. *I sure hope Maggie is right about my increased wealth.*

She had already bought the ingredients for her *Mama Llama Munchie Mix*, so she set about combining the corn chips, pretzel sticks, crunchy cereal squares, and mixed nuts into large zipper lock bags. She would add golden raisins and chocolate chips just before serving.

A shadow fell across Tommie's notepad. Looking up, she locked eyes with her new friend Aubrey Rush. Aubrey had been helpful in the investigation into the death of Veranell Collins.

"Aubrey! It's so good to see you. What's happening in the world of antiques and farm animals?"

Aubrey laughed, squinting her dark brown eyes. Her chestnut-colored ponytail bobbed. "Things are great. Antiques are selling, and farm animals are reproducing."

"And Levi Muller?"

"*Not* reproducing, Tommie, but there may be another engagement before long."

"No way! Aubrey, I can't tell you how happy that makes me. After what we've all gone through since Easter, I'm so ready for good news. Speaking of news, you heard what happened yesterday, I guess?"

"I did. Levi and I couldn't go, but word travels fast in a small town. Are you and Holmes investigating?"

"Duh. You know we are. Do you know anything that might help us?"

Aubrey scrunched up her mouth and drew her brows down. "Not really, Tommie. But I know it's hard to find out what happened to one victim, not to mention three. Is there a suspect?"

Tommie frowned. "Unfortunately, yes. Mrs. Gertrudis Padilla has motive and means to poison all three men."

"Poison again? That seems to be a common thread in deaths, of late."

"Yeah. But I don't believe she did it. I think there was a rush to judgment with her like there was with me. You know. 'Oh, the herbalist must've done it' kind of mentality. And her daughter has some strong motive, too. My head's kinda spinning with this one."

"Can I offer you a suggestion? I'm not a criminalist, but I am a pragmatist. When I have a multi-step problem to solve, I make a chart."

"Finbar and I do our case files in chart form."

"Let me amend that. I make tables and graphic illustrations. You must've done them as a teacher. Flow charts, graphs, Venn diagrams, radial charts. You know what I mean. Get your PowerPoint program out and make up some SmartArt graphics. Sometimes a picture works better than words."

"Dangit, girl! That's a great idea. I'm a visual person, and I love to 'colorize' things to make them stand out. And I can create the heck out of PowerPoint presentations. That might just work."

"Super. Do I get a commission?"

Tommie laughed aloud. "No commission, but I'll give you tea for life! By the way, why don't you bring Levi's granddaughters out to the Mother's Day Tea on Sunday?"

"I'm not a mother or a grandmother."

"Maybe not yet, but I predict you may be soon."

"Maybe, and I'll be the best Jewish Mennonite you've ever known. Now, how about some of that free tea you've promised me?"

"Teach me the Hebrew word for 'cheers'?"

"*L'Chayim.* It means 'to life.' May yours be long, Tommie Watson," Aubrey said with a smile.

"*L'Chayim* to you, too, Aubrey Rush ... the future Aubrey Muller."

Chapter Sixteen

FINBAR got an early start on breakfast the following day. He sent Sherlock out through the doggie door to collect Tommie at 7:30. She stumbled into his kitchen moments later, her face shining and her miniscule amount of makeup appropriate for a woman of her age. She wore a pair of scrubs patterned with colorful geometric shapes. A fresh mug of tea was waiting at her place at the table, along with the morning's fare: *Boxty with Fried Eggs and Black Pudding*, brown bread, Wexford cheese, and a side of pork 'n' beans. Tommie gratefully ate everything except the beans, which didn't appeal to her idea of breakfast food.

"Ready for today's interviews, missus?" Finbar asked after putting the empty plates in the sink to soak.

"Yep. Back to Greenleaf. I've got the addresses for all the food vendors." She tallied them up quickly. "León

and Letitia Luz and Jorge and Soledad Fuentes are retired. We can visit them in their homes. Hector Flores works in town, but Carmine should be home unless she is substitute teaching. Padre Juan Sanchez will be at the church, *Iglesia de Santa Maria*. That's six interviews in Greenleaf. Then we can come back and see Hector at the Rx-All or the Winn Dixie. We've already talked to Gertrudis and Lara. That only leaves you, me, and our Fab Four. Elaine said they would meet us tomorrow for lunch. I'm ready."

"Lovely. I'll meet ye at yer car in a shake." He turned to the dogs. "Here, lads. D'you wants the leftovers?"

Three sets of tails wagged happily.

"Finbar, please don't give them the beans. You know what that does to them."

Finbar pursed his thin lips and raised his brows. "I knows, but they does like them and we'll be out and about. The smell will be gone by the time we return."

Tommie groaned and made her way out the front door to her car.

"Now, lads. I know ye loves them, so I'll not deprive ye. Besides, 'better out than in,' I always says."

Leaving the dogs to their feast, he exited the duplex and climbed in the passenger seat of Tommie's SUV. Seeing her scowl, he shrugged his shoulders and grinned.

"At least it's *your* house they'll stink up," she said.

"Maybe. *Yer* dog portal is open, too, ye know."

Tommie glowered at him and shook her head. "You won't do, Finbar Holmes. You won't do."

He laughed aloud. "Yer right, lad. Tell me, what're yer thoughts this morning about the investigation?"

"I think we've got to try and rule out these vendors. From what I hear so far, Both Larry and Jimmy Clay were consummate womanizers, only Larry had more finesse. Jimmy was bad in all kinds of ways."

"And the doctor?"

"He had his own thing going on with women and a sketchy medical acumen."

"Not very likable chaps, were they?"

"They were definitely lacking in character."

"What did yer detective mate tell ye last night?"

"Pretty much the same thing. There were lots of motives to get rid of them. Our problem is finding the one person who had the most motive to kill all three of them."

"Aye. 'Tis a daunting task, but Holmes and Watson are up to the challenge."

"If you say so."

Tommie pulled her car up to the curb in front of a wood framed house painted a pale yellow with an emerald green front door.

"This is where León and Letitia Luz live," she said as they stepped up on the cement front porch and knocked.

A woman of medium height and weight with short pewter grey hair opened the door. When she saw Tommie, she broke into a smile and stepped out to clasp her hands.

"*Señora* Tommie. How good to see you. What brings you to my house? Are you out of *queso fundido*

picante salsa so quickly?"

Tommie snickered. "No, Letitia. Not quite yet. My friend Finbar and I are driving around town, and we thought we'd stop in to say 'hello' to you and León."

Letitia clucked her tongue with a *tsk-tsk* sound, and her hazelnut eyes sparkled. "Your reputation is well known in Floral County, Tommie. You have come to ask questions. Am I a suspect?"

"No, no. I apologize for the ruse. Yes. We are asking questions of everyone who had a *cabina* at the event last Sunday."

"But I am confused. We were questioned by the police that night."

"Ahhh, we are doing our own questioning … just to cover all the bases."

"I see. Then come inside while I go get León away from the car he is tinkering with. Imagine, 70 years old and still thinks he is a mechanic. *Por favor.* Please make yourselves at home."

Letitia ushered them into a cozy living room. The walls were covered with vibrant fruit and flower still life paintings. In the far corner, a sewing machine was set up beside a bookcase filled with fabrics, patterns, and notions.

"Do ye sew, missus?" Finbar asked.

Letitia beamed. "I used to be a fine seamstress, but at 68, arthritis keeps me from doing the embroidery work I used to pride myself on. Now, I make simpler clothing items for my friends and their children."

"M'late wife Mary used to sew," he said, making the sign of the cross and kissing his thumb. "I've always felt needlework 'tis the art of a talented, genteel woman."

"*Gracias, señor* Holmes. I will get my husband."

She exited the back door, and Tommie noticed her posture, which was already perfect, seemed to straighten even more. *Way to go, Finbar. Always charming the ladies.*

Letitia returned, followed by her husband, León. Tommie was struck by the disparity in the two. Although they both roughly stood the same height and carried similar weight, the man was bent and stooped. *Must be from years of hovering over the engines of cars,* she deduced. Despite his appearance, he had a strong, firm handshake.

"Good day t'ye, sir," Finbar said.

"*Buenos días* to you both. Letitia tells me you have questions that will help find the killers of these men," he said, running his hand through his thin salt and pepper hair.

"Er. What makes ye think the men were killed?" Finbar asked, sitting forward in his chair.

León and his wife regarded him from the sofa.

"Because," León said, "you wouldn't be asking questions if they died of natural causes."

Tommie nodded in agreement. "True. Did you think, at the time, that they were natural causes?"

Letitia smirked. "*Señora* Tommie. Did you?"

"No, I really didn't. It was too coincidental for them to die one after the other like that. What I'm wondering is if you saw or heard anything that would lead

you to believe someone may have done it. I'm sure the police already asked you, but sometimes we remember things later that we overlooked in the heat of the moment."

León smiled wanly. "We may be older, but we have lived through many things, good and bad. They were *hombres malos*. Bad men. None of those men were held in very high regard in our community, not even the doctor."

"Especially the doctor." Letitia's face darkened beneath lowered brows.

"Why the doctor?" Tommie asked.

"He killed our friend." León's voice was harsh.

"Are ye speaking of Mr. Padilla?" Finbar asked.

"*Sí.* Salvador was one of my best friends. He had a bad heart, and instead of fixing it, Dr. Frank made it worse by directing the pharmacist to overmedicate him."

"Ye know that for certain, d'you?"

León's hands clinched into fists. "I am positive he did. Then he got that fancy Lassiter man to be his lawyer. He ended up not held responsible and didn't pay anything to Gertrudis or Lara, and they needed the help."

"So, Larry Clay was partly responsible for Mr. Padilla's death?" Tommie asked.

"Of course, he was. He knew the prescription was wrong, but he pushed it through because he was Dr. Frank's man. In return, the doctor convinced Mr. Beadwell to promote Mr. Clay over Hector," Letitia said.

"Hector ... Flores?"

"*Sí.* Hector had worked at the Rx-All many years

more than Mr. Clay, but he was passed over because he questioned the medicine dosage Dr. Frank prescribed."

"What?"

"Hector said it was too strong, but Larry Clay insisted it was correct. Salvador died from it, I'm sure of that. Then Hector was punished for not going along with Dr. Frank. They cut back his hours. I blame Tom Beadwell for being such a coward. He should have known better, but he was depending on Dr. Frank for referring patients to his pharmacy. Hector had to take a second job at the Winn Dixie pharmacy to make up the lost wages."

"Seems a nasty business with the doctor and his chemist. 'Tis a pity yer friends have suffered," Finbar said.

"They are good friends. Many good people have suffered at the hands of the *hombres malos*," León said.

"Anyone else we know?" Tommie asked.

"You know Jorge and Soledad Fuentes. You met them Sunday. Theirs was the *sopes de ternera con frijoles negros cabana*."

"The beef and black bean tortillas. I remember. What happened to them?"

"Jorge was a teller at the First Bank of Floribunda until Dr. Frank prescribed the wrong medication for his heart condition. Larry Clay also filled the prescription. Jorge is no longer able to work because his heart was damaged by the pills." He shook his head.

"And Soledad had to take a job as a part-time cashier at the Winn Dixie," Letitia added.

"Did he also try to sue?"

"No. Dr. Frank and Larry Clay convinced him that the medicine was right, but he took it wrong."

"D'you mean to say they bullied him into believing it was his own fault?" Finbar asked.

"They did. And to make it worse, Larry's brother Jimmy came to the house and said he would do harm to their daughter, Lorena, if they tried to sue his brother."

Tommie's mouth snapped open. "What? Like a common thug? Like the Mafia or something?"

"It is as you say, Tommie. It was like something from the television. But, before you go wondering, Jorge Fuentes would never try to kill anyone. You cannot think of him as a suspect ... he is a victim."

"And there are many, many more who suffered from these three men. I hate to say, but it is a blessing that they are dead." León patted his wife's hand and rose from the sofa. "So, now, I will excuse myself to the back yard and continue my work. Engines are simple, straightforward things. Unlike men."

Chapter Seventeen

TOMMIE AND FINBAR concluded their short interviews with Jorge and Soledad Fuentes. Jorge was a tall but pudgy 62-year-old man with a good sense of humor. His wife Soledad was a short, full-figured 60-year-old woman with a quick laugh and a humble, homespun manner. They corroborated the stories of their neighbors and confirmed that they dropped their lawsuit mainly because of Jimmy Clay's threat to attack their daughter. Fortunately, the girl was away in her last year of graduate school and was far from danger; however, Tommie noted the pained expressions they held when they spoke of her.

Their last stop in Greenleaf was at *Iglesia de Santa Maria*. The septuagenarian priest, Padre Juan Sanchez, reminded Tommie of a character in a spaghetti-Western, with his round belly and "monk's bowl"—bald headed on

top with a fringe of white hair that circled beneath the shiny pate. Though his brown eyes were kind within his pudgy adobe-colored face, he proved to be very circumspect regarding his parishioners and humbly, yet firmly, declined to discuss the people in his church. Nor would he give the slightest hint of an opinion on Dr. Norman Frank, Larry Clay, or Jimmy Clay. Hitting a brick wall, Tommie and Finbar thanked him for his time and left town.

"Finbar," Tommie said as they drove back toward Floribunda, "I'm seeing a pattern in this community. Dr. Frank gave sketchy medical care, Larry Clay dispensed incorrect medication, and Jimmy Clay terrorized all the women. Would you say that's accurate?"

"I would, indeed. 'Tis a wonder they were not killed long before now. It seems quite a few people had motive to do them in. What d'you think we should make of it?"

"I'd really like to talk to Hector, but I don't want to meet him at the Rx-All tomorrow. I don't want to run into Tom Beadwell. It seems he's as shifty as his ex-wife, Linda, and his current girlfriend, Eva Edgerton. What's wrong with people anymore?"

"I dunno, lad. Shall we try to catch Mr. Flores now while he's working at the Winn Dixie?"

"Let's. And while we're there, I need some supplies for Sunday's Mother's Day Tea Party. A lot of supplies."

"I fear ye've bitten off more than ye can chew with this luncheon, Thomasina. Will ye be able to get all the

sandwiches done in time, or will ye need m'help?"

"Are you kidding. Of course, I'll need your help!"

As they pulled into the parking lot, Tommie's cellphone rang.

"Oh. That's Earl. You go on in and start with Hector. I'll be right there," she said.

"Righto." He gave her a tip of an imaginary hat.

"Hey, Earl," Tommie said as Finbar exited. "Whatcha doing today?"

"Hey there, darlin'. I reckon I'm doing the same thing you are."

"Um. I'm just at Winn Dixie getting some food for Sunday's tea party."

"Um hmm. And is Holmes with you?"

"Well, yeah."

"Winn Dixie, huh? Would you by chance be there to interview Soledad Fuentes?"

"Why no. Why would I interview her?"

Earl guffawed. "Tommie, she was at the event, and she would be on your list."

"Well, for your information, we are not here to speak with Soledad."

"Then, since you're obviously still in your car, Holmes must be inside talking to Hector Flores."

Tommie fish mouthed for a moment before she recovered. "M-maybe."

"Tommie ..."

"Earl ..."

"Lord, woman. Can't you please play straight with me? Remember, I didn't tell you not to investigate ..."

"You just told me to be careful."

"That's right. So, enlighten me. Who's number one on your suspect list now?"

"Earl, I'm gonna give you the honest truth. There were so many people with motives to kill any and all of those men, it's shocking! But after talking with them, I don't think *any* of them we've interviewed would have done it. Do *you* have a prime suspect, and can you tell me?"

"Mmmm. Darlin', you know I can't divulge that information, but if I were you, I would make a date with Don, Henry, and the sisters very soon. Tomorrow, if you can manage it. They know more than they are admitting to me. Much more. And don't forget, Elaine and Susan were married to two of the dead men. If anyone can get them to open up, it's you and Holmes."

"You're not telling me to be careful."

"With those four? Absolutely not. But maybe I should warn them about you, my love."

Tommie grinned, feeling warm and fluttery inside. "Earl Petry. The things you say. Are we still on for tomorrow night?"

"Yup. What're you in the mood for?"

"You. I'm in the mood for you."

"I'll be dessert, darlin'. How about dinner at The Fallen Oak? Pick you up at seven."

"Seven, it is, and dessert afterward."

"You bet. Now get yourself inside and collaborate with your partner. I'll see you tomorrow."

Tommie disconnected the phone and entered the grocery store. She saw Finbar and Hector sitting on a bench outside the pharmacy counter. They rose when she approached them.

"No need for that, fellas. Hi, Hector. I hope you're doing all right," she said.

"I'm fine, Ms. Watson. Here, please take my seat. I've got to keep an eye on the counter anyway."

Tommie gratefully accepted the seat on the bench. She stretched her leg out and painfully rotated her ankle. Noticing Hector watching her, she slowly pulled her leg back and scrutinized him while he and Finbar talked.

Hector Flores was 64, carried himself well, and seemed relatively fit for his age. His soft brown eyes shone behind black frame glasses, and from time to time he reached up and patted his fine, mostly grey, hair. He had a friendly demeanor and a ready smile.

"...and yer relationship to the Padilla family is what, exactly?" Finbar asked.

"I have been friends with the Padillas since high school. Salvador and I were classmates, and Gertrudis was a couple of years behind us. Lara is my godchild, and Dearcilla is my great godchild. I love them very much."

"Tell me what happened with yer position at the Rx-All, Hector. I heard ye got demoted."

Hector blew out his breath, and his lips made a

buzzing sound. "That has been bad for my family. Carmine has severe arthritis. Her medication is awfully expensive. I needed the promotion to help pay for her treatments. Dr. Norman Frank was notorious for misdiagnosing conditions and prescribing medicines that contraindicated each other. I had to be so careful to compare every prescription he wrote with the patient's chart to be sure there would be no adverse reactions. I cannot tell you how many times I had to call his office for alternate medicine. I kept detailed records of every person who used the pharmacy." He darted his eyes around to be sure he was not being overheard. "I even dispensed compounds and medications that would be better tolerated."

"Do you mean to say you dispensed your own prescriptions?" Tommie asked.

"Oh, no. I gave people over-the-counter options and wholistic alternatives. Like for your ankle. I can suggest an inexpensive compound that will help with that swelling."

"Thank you. Did that go over well with the alternative medicines?"

"With the customers it did. Not so much with Tom Beadwell. He owns the drug store, you know. Prescription pharmaceuticals bring in quite a bit more money. But I did it for the wellbeing of the people. The cost of many medications is prohibitive. Greenleaf, in particular, does not have a wealthy population. Cottonfield is a farming community, so there's not much money there, either. I tried to make medicine more affordable."

"That's good of ye to have that concern," Finbar said. "After all, the chemist knows best what will or will not work."

"Exactly. Except Dr. Frank and Tom Beadwell had something going, I believe, that was mutually beneficial, money-wise. That's why, when I pointed out the prescription for Salvador was dangerously high, I was told to mind my own business. Larry Clay jumped in and insisted the dosage was correct. Tom said he liked Larry's 'initiative,' and that's why he got the promotion. I had worked at the Rx-All 14 years. Larry Clay had only been there three years. Truth be told, Larry was Dr. Frank's and Tom's yes-man."

"I'm sorry, Hector. What did you do?"

"There was nothing I *could* do. To make matters worse, Dr. Frank threatened to have my license revoked for illegally prescribing medicine. My only alternative was to suck it up and find another part-time job to meet the bills. Tom even turned a blind eye to Larry taking pills from the pharmacy without recording them on the books."

"D'you mean he medicated himself from the stock on the shelves?"

"No, not himself ... his worthless, piece of trash brother." Hector's jaw clenched.

"Ye didn't like him, eh?"

"Why on earth would anyone like him, much less sleep with him?" Hector pinched his nose as though smelling something pungent.

"D'you know anyone who had sex with him?"

Hector scoffed. "Plenty. We could've done a good business on meds for herpes and other intimate contact diseases just because of him alone. You'd be surprised at the women he bedded."

"In this day and age, did the man not get himself checked out at a clinic for sex diseases?" Finbar asked.

"You'd think so, but no. Big brother Larry gave him meds every time he had a flare-up. He spread more than blue eyes and dimples around."

Tommie sat up and leaned forward. "Hector, what do you think about all three of those men dying from complications of *Digitalis*?"

Hector stared at her. "What did you say?"

"*Digitalis*. That's the drug that was found in their bloodstream. How d'you think it got there?" Finbar said.

Hector leaned against the counter, swallowed repeatedly, and swiped his hair back from his forehead. "I ... I don't have a clue, Mr. Holmes. As far as I'm aware, none of them had a heart condition."

"Could the drug possibly enter the bloodstream transdermally through the skin?" Tommie asked.

"That's not likely, but I suppose it could happen."

"D'you think the *Digitalis* could have come from the Rx-All ... or from here?" Finbar asked.

Hector drew himself up and stood stiffly. He smoothed his white lab coat and adjusted his glasses. "I honestly could not say. I don't have any way of knowing

how or why they ingested *Digitalis.* But, if you two will please excuse me, my break is over, and I have to get back to work. Good-bye."

Finbar and Tommie watched as Hector Flores strode off behind the counter and disappeared into the office within the pharmacy. The exchange had abruptly taken a left turn, leaving Holmes and Watson wondering what Hector Flores had to hide.

Chapter Eighteen

TOMMIE was surprised to see the gossipy quartet walk into Watson's Reme-Teas late that afternoon.

"Hey, ya'll! I thought we were having lunch tomorrow. I didn't expect to see you today, but I'm delighted. What can I get for you?" she said.

"Sister and I will have the *Lemon-Lime Llama Tea,* Tommie," Susan said. "We brought some *Lunar Lemon Squares* from The Lunch Pad, and we'll share with you."

"Yum! Two teas coming up, on the house. My treat. How about you, Henry? Don?"

"Is Finbar next door yet?" Don asked.

"Oh, yeah. He's prepping, as usual."

"Can Henry and I go over?"

"Sure, you can. Go on through the connecting door. Here you go, ladies." Tommie put two extra-large

mugs on saucers for the sisters while the men headed for Caife Caife Holmes.

"Tommie, can you sit with us for a while? The shop's not busy right now," Elaine asked.

"I'd love to." Tommie grabbed her bottled water and followed the women to a table near the display window. "What brings you in today?"

"We won't be able to have lunch tomorrow," Susan said. "Sister's got to be at Lassiter's Law Offices for the reading of the will."

"Whose will?"

"My late ex-husband's will. Norman," Elaine said.

"Really? Are you …? I mean, do you think …? Um. Why do you have to be there, Elaine? Haven't you been divorced from him for like seven or eight years?"

"Yes, but I got a call from Simone saying my presence was required."

"Simone Lorence? That must've been awkward."

"It was," Susan said. "What with that little hussy being the reason they divorced. But she's Lassiter's legal secretary, so I guess it was her job to call."

"Sister, she was not the only reason we divorced, but she was the main one. I'm going to tell you some things, Tommie, because you're my friend, and you need to know them for your investigation," Elaine said. "And sister, I'll thank you not to butt in while I'm talking, or I might lose my train of thought."

Susan pulled her fingers across her mouth to "zip

her lips," while Tommie nodded and sipped her water.

Elaine sucked in a deep breath. "Norman was my second husband. I have a grown daughter from my first marriage to the psychiatrist Dr. Nelson Stone, but Norman and I had no children. We divorced after he began seeing Simone Lorence. Simone is Harvey Lassiter's legal secretary. She came to Floribunda about eight years ago, supposedly from France by way of Miami. Norman was involved in a malpractice suit at the time, and Simone spent way too many late hours 'helping' him with the case, so things progressed between the two of them."

"Meaning they were sleeping together," Susan said.

"Shhh. Norman was acquitted of the charge ..."

"...but not the affair."

"Sister, please. Tommie, I knew he was guilty. I overheard him talking to Larry Clay when he and Susan were over for dinner one night. Norman and Larry were in the study. I went to knock on the door to call them to the table, and I heard them discussing how they needed to be more careful in the future, that they almost got caught. I was standing at the door with my hand raised when Norman pushed it open. Larry scooted around me in a hurry, but Norman just stared at me with no emotion whatsoever."

"Larry was such a spineless coward."

"For cripes sake, Sister." Elaine gave her a scathing look before turning to face Tommie again. "Norman didn't hem or haw or try to explain. He looked me square in the

eye and said, 'Elaine. I'm divorcing you for another woman. If you're smart, you'll stay quiet and accept a very generous alimony.' The generous alimony was $10,000 a month."

Tommie's mouth hung open. "He ... what?"

"He paid me $10,000 a month for the past seven years. Tommie, I'm so ashamed. It was hush money, but it was so much more than I earned at the bank."

"But $10,000 a month? How come you still worked at the bank?"

"Because I was afraid. Afraid that if I quit, somebody would find out. You know, like the IRS."

"Didn't you claim it on your tax return?"

Elaine cleared her throat. "It was mostly in cash."

Tommie sat back in her chair and blinked at her friend. "Cash. That's $120,000 a year."

"Before you get the wrong idea about me, I want you to know that the divorce agreement stipulated $3,000 a month, but Norman paid me another $7,000 under the table. I kept the monthly check, and I claimed it on my tax returns, but I anonymously donated the cash to a different charity each month."

"Well, I guess that makes it OK." Tommie's voice was quiet, and she avoided Elaine's eyes.

Elaine was near tears, but she kept her chin up. "And every month, I deposit $1,500 into a savings account at the bank for Gertrudis Padilla and her family."

"Does Gertrudis know about the money for Salvador's death?"

"She does," Elaine confirmed. "I told her I thought my husband was negligent, even though the court didn't. It was my way of easing my conscience and making Norman pay, in some respect."

"I ... I don't know what to say, Elaine. In theory, I guess you only kept half of your alimony payment and donated half to Gertrudis. And I suppose the rest could be considered a 'gift.' What do you think is in the will?"

"I don't know, but Norman had a notarized agreement made up by Lassiter and signed by Simone, that the payments would continue as long as he was alive. Now that he's dead, I'm betting the agreement is null and void."

"Possibly. You say Simone knew this? She signed as a witness. So ... if Dr. Frank died, you'd be cut off."

Susan interrupted. "Yes! Don't you see? If Elaine is out of the pocket, then maybe Simone is his estate or insurance beneficiary, and if the woman thinks that, she may try to go after Elaine!"

"Whoa. That sounds like a motive to me," Tommie said. "She kills him, so she gets his money. And, yes, I could absolutely see her not wanting Elaine to have any more money from his estate. But why wait so long?"

"Maybe Norman was changing his will. I don't know. Do you think I have a motive, Tommie?" Elaine said. "I get nothing if he's dead."

"Looks like you're clear ... of murder, at least. I don't know about the cash money. What if Simone informs the IRS? What'll you do?"

Elaine shrugged. "I don't know. Play dumb?"

"We were in banking, sister. How could we be dumb about something like that?" Susan said.

"Oh, no!" Tommie's eyebrows arched up. "Susan, you knew about it and didn't come forward to report it. That makes you complicit!"

"It does in more than one way. I knew Larry was involved in the seedy business, but I said nothing, even when he barely gave me any alimony when we divorced."

"Because you didn't want to hurt your sister. I get it. What happened between you and Larry?"

Susan scoffed. "Larry was a womanizer. I knew it, but I loved him. I also had a daughter from my first marriage, but I couldn't have any more children of my own, and that was a major source of contention. He didn't give two figs for my daughter. I heard through the grapevine that he was fooling around with a teenage girl. That was more than I could stomach. I couldn't be married to a pedophile, so I divorced him."

Tommie blanched at the thought of the man preying on young girls. She sloshed water around in her dry mouth and kept her eyes on Susan.

"Larry paid me a little bit of alimony until he started going with Katherine Howell, then it began to dwindle away until he quit altogether. But I couldn't say anything because he knew I had the dirt on him for the death of Salvador Padilla and Elaine's financial agreement with Norman. Then, Katherine got pregnant, or so she said,

and he wanted that baby, so he married her to give the baby his name. As soon as that happened, Katherine conveniently 'lost' the baby."

"I heard she had a hysterectomy," Tommie said.

Elaine sniffed. "So did we, but she kept that fact from Larry. He still thought she might bear him a child."

"Sister, it's your turn to be quiet. This is *my* story," Susan said. "Anyhow, he ran around on me. I don't think he consciously tried to father other children, but I know he fathered at least one. For some reason, the Clay men have dominant blue eye and dimple genes."

"Yep. I've heard that. It seems Jimmy Clay has a bunch of his progeny around the county, like that sweet little Dearci Padilla," Tommie said.

Elaine and Susan both stared at Tommie with pained expressions.

Tommie looked at them in confusion. "Isn't that right? That's what Earl told me. She's definitely got his blue eyes and dimples."

"Oh, Tommie. You've got it wrong. I'm sorry, but we lied to Earl about that," Elaine stated.

"Why?"

"To protect my sister. I don't want her involved."

"I don't understand."

"It's so I don't have a motive, Tommie," Susan said. "Dearci's a Clay, for sure, but her father was Larry."

Chapter Nineteen

FINBAR and his friends Henry and Don sipped their Irish coffees and talked politics, poker, and potential murderers. They agreed that Hector Flores was a likely suspect, in addition to Gertrudis and/or Lara Padilla.

"My money is on Hector, although I have a hard time believing he would do something so premeditated," Don said. "He's such an easygoing guy."

"True, but when people are pushed to the brink, they don't think as clearly as they should," Henry said.

"D'you think either of the women could commit such a crime? And how d'you think they'd get the chemist's pills? I can see the herbs, but not the *Digitalis* itself," Finbar pointed out.

Don grimaced. "Well, I hate to say it, but I heard the girl had been seen with the pharmacist on several

occasions when she was a teenager. She used to work as a cashier at the Rx-All back then. Larry had a roving eye, and she was quite the pretty little thing. I observed her flirting with him one day when I was picking up a prescription."

Finbar pursed his lips. "D'you think she had a fling with yer man when she was but a girl?"

"It's possible, Holmes. I heard that the younger brother, Jimmy, caught her when she was walking home one night and attacked her." Henry was clearly embarrassed.

"Aye, he raped her, I was told." Finbar shook his head from side to side. "Disgusting brute. He should've been arrested by the *Gardai.*"

"That would be the police, Don."

"Thank you, Henry. I knew that. She wouldn't be the first to fall victim to Jimmy Clay. Henry dated Jo for a while. Tell Finbar what Jo revealed to you."

Henry's face colored. "She ... she told me in confidence, but I think she wouldn't mind you knowing, Holmes. She likes you and Tommie a lot. Jo said Jimmy beat her up regularly, and he would go out and seduce other women and then come home and describe the encounters to her. She had the classic abused wife syndrome. We didn't date long because she suffered some lingering trauma from it. PTSD, I think. I'm so glad she and Santino are engaged. He'll be good for her."

"Aye. Santino is a good lad. He'll protect her right well." Finbar patted his friend gently on the back.

"Maybe too well." Don leaned in with his

eyebrows raised. "Finbar, did you know Santino and Leo were street fighters in Mexico?"

"Were they, now? Did they fight for money?"

"Yes, they did. They also were like the Mexican equivalent of enforcers for a gang. Santino was arrested and held for questioning in the death of a man he beat up."

"What're ye saying? Santino killed a man with his bare fists? I find that hard to swallow."

"It's true, Holmes." Henry nodded his head. "Leo told me, when he came over to our booth Sunday after Jimmy bothered Jo at Lara's booth, that he has to keep watch on his brother when he gets mad. He said Santino's fists could be considered lethal weapons."

"D'you think he could kill a man with one punch? D'you think he meant to kill Jimmy Clay that night?"

Henry and Don both pulled their shoulders up to their ears. Finbar drained his cup and sat back in the chair. "Who else knows about their street fighting history?"

"*We* haven't told *anyone* ... except you. We like the Alvarez brothers," Henry said solemnly.

"For cripes sake, Finbar, they saved you and Tommie from being burned alive, and they repaired your shops almost singlehandedly. I don't think murder's even a possibility," Don said.

"But a temper can be a nasty thing, m'friends, if it's not kept in check, and in the heat of passion. For the time being, let's be sure to keep this amongst ourselves. I has to tell Thomasina, though, but not her beau. D'you agree?"

Don and Henry nodded and continued sipping their coffees while Holmes refreshed his from the hot pot. They sat silently, mulling over their thoughts, until the connecting door opened, and Tommie, Elaine, and Susan entered the café.

"Halloo, sisters," Finbar called. "Will ye join us in a coffee?"

"No thank you, Finbar. We've come to collect Donnie and Henry. We're going out to Floribunda Steak House for dinner," Elaine said.

"We had originally wanted to try the new place, *Mucho Mexicali,* but nobody's much in the mood for Mexican food today. Wish you could join us," Susan said.

"Never ye mind, ladies. Perhaps by the weekend. Will we be seeing ye for dinner on Saturday next? I'm preparing a delicious *Tamale Pie* with Thomasina's *Easy Enchilada Sauce,* a creamy melt-in-yer-mouth *Mexican Flan* for dessert, and a special *Mexican Coffee* with cinnamon, brown sugar, orange peel, and chocolate."

The sisters tittered and clapped their hands.

Henry wrapped his long arms around a sister on either side. "We'll be there, Holmes. Same table as usual."

Tommie opened the front door for them and turned the sign to OPEN. For the next couple of hours, there was a steady stream of customers buying Irish coffee and thick slices of brown soda bread with *Kerrygold* butter and Wexford cheese.

Holmes was in his element, chatting with patrons,

pouring coffee, and slicing bread, hot from the oven. While he schmoozed, Tommie perched on a high stool and manned the cash register. In between orders, she scribbled on a yellow legal pad, drawing circles and lines, and writing notes. When, at last, the customers dwindled, and the sign was switched back to CLOSED, Finbar stepped up and glanced at her drawings.

"What're ye doing, missus? I seen ye working on yer sketches."

"I'm trying out something a little different. Aubrey suggested it. I used to do these with the kids at school to help them focus on story writing. We called them story webs." She held the pad up for him to see. "It's actually a radial graph. I put our victim's name in a circle in the middle of the page. This one is Dr. Norman Frank. Then I put lines radiating out from his name. I end each line in a circle, and in each one, I write the name of a suspect. I'm leaving plenty of empty circles in case we find other suspects that seem promising."

"What's the writing beside the circles?"

"Pertinent information, like motive."

"Ah. I see. What're the circles ye have in that box and that cluster on the side?"

"Those are persons of interest that could possibly be suspects, but I haven't determined any motive yet."

"Good on ye, Thomasina. It looks easy to understand. Let me see. Ye have six suspect names in the circles. Gertrudis Padilla, Katherine Clay, Simone Lorence,

Lara Padilla, Hector Flores. Wait. Is that Elaine Frank?"

"Um. Yes. I have some news for you. We'll have to talk about it when we get home."

"Then I suggest we do a quick wash-up and get to the house. The dogs'll be wanting a snack, too."

"I'm all done next door. Just need to grab my keys."

"Lovely. I'll leave the cups in the sink to soak and finish them off tomorrow. I'm afraid I have a bit of news for ye, as well, that's very troubling, indeed."

Chapter Twenty

TOMMIE lay in bed staring at the ceiling as Zed snored on the pillow beside her. Sleep had not come easily, and she had awakened many times from disturbing dreams, the last one in which multiple people collapsed and died in a heap at her feet. The faces of her friends appeared in a montage, interspersed with those of past and present suspects, masked physicians, heaps of pills and medicine bottles, and gangs fighting with fists and knives and chains. Her waking mind was filled with charts and radial graphs and lists.

The light filtering through the mini binds gradually brightened, and she glanced at the wall clock. Finbar would undoubtedly be up and beginning a lavish breakfast for the two of them, so she sighed and extricated her feet from beneath Red to head for the shower.

Twenty minutes later, she walked through her

neighbor's kitchen door. Zed and Red entered behind her and greeted Sherlock as Finbar greeted Tommie.

"Halloo, missus. Ye've got good timing. The black pudding's crispy, the eggs are runny, the bread's hot from the oven, and yer mug is waiting for ye to serve the tea."

Tommie mumbled and sat down, pouring a generous splash of milk into Finbar's mug before filling it with the hot tea. She added a spoonful of *Honey-Honey* to her mug and inhaled the delicious, sweet scent of the brew.

Finbar stabbed a round of the fried sausage and loaded up the back of his fork with a smear of egg yolk.

"Ye look a might haggard this morning, lad. Did ye not sleep well?"

"I didn't. Bad dreams. This case is really kicking my butt. I can't figure out who or what happened. At this point, it seems everybody and their brother wanted to kill these men ... and, sad to say, I don't blame them."

"There's reason enough for anybody to have done the deed but putting them at the scene with the means and the motive is our task. 'Tis like a crossword. Ye get one letter wrong, and the whole puzzle is out of sorts. D'you understand?"

"I do. Gads, it's frustrating. I thought I was better than this at figuring things out."

"Perhaps ye need to rest from going out and talking with the last few suspects. D'you want to stay home and work on yer computer charts? I can go on m'own today."

"Who's left to interview?"

"There's the two who lived with the dead men. Mrs. Katherine Clay and Ms. Simone Lorence."

"And Jo Clay."

"And Ms. Jo Clay. Why don't ye call her on the phone and speak with her, Thomasina? To m'own thinking, she's not so much a viable suspect. But, sure, sure. We've got to leave no stone unturned, and she may provide some evidence to exonerate Santino."

At the mention of the older Alvarez brother, Tommie grew agitated. "I refuse to believe Santino killed Jimmy Clay . . . even accidentally." She sat up straight in her chair. "I'm going to call Sandy."

"Well done, lad. The coroner can surely put yer mind at ease. Good on you, Thomasina."

"Yeah, I think I'll investigate from home this morning and meet you at your shop later on. You don't mind talking with the other two ladies?"

"Nah. They're just women, after all."

Tommie glared at him. "Finbar, up to now, all the killers we've caught have been women!"

Finbar's eyes twinkled. "I knew I'd goad ye to rise to the occasion. You work yer magic on paper, and I'll set out on foot. Leave yer plate, lad, and I'll put it to rinse."

"Oh, by the way, don't forget that Simone will be at the lawyer's office for the reading of the will. I figure they'll be done by 10:00 or so. Katherine's probably not gone back to work, yet. She'll be making arrangements for Larry's funeral. You might catch her at home."

"Ne'er ye fret, dear. I can manage."

"I have no doubt. Little boys, y'all can spend the morning with me. See you this afternoon, Finbar."

Tommie left her empty plate on the table and returned to her side of the duplex, leaving Finbar to feed the scraps to the dogs and set the dishes in the sink. A few minutes later, she heard the *blam-blam-blam* of the doggie door as the three happy pooches returned to her spare room office to roost.

She gathered her loose papers into a heap and deposited them beside the computer. Checking her wall clock, she decided to wait until 8:30 to call the coroner's office. In the meantime, she booted up her laptop and pulled up the last PowerPoint slide she had worked on.

The flow chart appeared as rectangles in eight columns of six. Between each rectangle was an arrow pointing to the next shape in line. Being a visually oriented former elementary school teacher, Tommie had assigned colors to each shape which corresponded to an action or event attributed to specific people. Everything pertaining to Dr. Norman Frank was black; Larry Clay was navy-blue; Jimmy Clay was light grey. The suspects were yellow, pink, green, orange, and purple. The couples—Dr. Frank, Simone, Larry, and Katherine—were represented as dark grey. Police were bright blue, including Earl. Sandy and the EMTs were brown. Finbar was peach, and Tommie herself was turquoise. The colors helped her focus more clearly.

Tommie traced the shapes in a snakelike pattern

from the first to the last. *This looks like a Disneyworld line, except the ride at the end is not going to be much fun.*

Because Finbar was of a more linear frame of mind, she opened a new document and listed the events numerically, as seen from her perspective.

1. Dr. Frank & Simone arrive (agitated)
2. Simone makes speech at bandstand
3. Meet up w/Larry & Katherine (arguing)
4. Couples buy food from vendors
5. Couples sit at table between Tommie & Gertrudis, across from Finbar.
6. Dearci brings *Pico de Gallo* bowls to the table
7. Couples eat food in strained silence
8. Jo visits Lara's booth

The next arrow pointed down and then to the left. Tommie continued the list.

9. Dearci hugs Jo; gives her salsa bowls
10. Jimmy harasses Jo
11. Jo cracks her bowl, slaps Jimmy
12. Jimmy drinks salsa from broken bowl
13. Santino threatens Jimmy
14. Jo pulls Santino away
15. Jimmy sits at table with couples
16. Larry gives him a beer

The next arrow pointed down, and then the boxes continued to the right.

17. Jimmy insults tablemates; drinks lots of beer
18. Santino & Leo help Don & Henry at booth

19. Jo visits soft drink booth

20. Jimmy follows Jo

21. Jimmy accosts Jo

22. Jo screams

23. Santino & Leo come running

24. Santino punches Jimmy

The arrow pointed down, and the row progressed to the left.

25. Jimmy knocked out

26. Leo checks Jimmy

27. JIMMY CLAY IS DEAD

28. Larry rises from table to see

29. Larry staggers & collapses

30. Katherine screams

31. Dr. Frank does CPR

32. LARRY CLAY IS DEAD

The arrow pointed down, then directed the boxes to the right.

33. Dr. Frank begins vomiting

34. Gertrudis gives him 2 potions

35. Dr. Frank keels over

36. Simone screams

37. Tommie does CPR

38. Finbar calls 9-1-1.

39. NORMAN FRANK IS DEAD

40. Tommie calls Earl.

The last arrow pointed down and finally took the row to the left.

41. Crime scene victims blocked off
42. Earl arrives w/Jenny & Dale
43. Floral County EMTs arrive
44. Sanderson Harper (coroner) arrives
45. All 3 victims checked
46. All 3 victims taken to morgue
47. Earl/Jenny/Dale question witnesses
48. OFFICIAL INVESTIGATION BEGINS

Tommie sat back and perused the list. Satisfied that it was an accurate representation of the events which took place, she checked the wall clock and picked up her cellphone. Sanderson Harper answered on the third ring.

"Well, cousin. How can I assist Holmes and Watson, Investigators this morning?

"Hey, Sandy. I have a few questions."

"Figured you would. Ask away."

"You're not gonna tell me it's confidential police business and none of mine?

"Would it matter?"

"No, of course not."

"Then fire away, Tommie."

"All right. First of all, I'm wondering about the injuries Jimmy Clay sustained when he was punched."

"Heck of a punch."

"Did it kill him? I mean, was that the main cause of his death?"

"Well, it certainly didn't help. But no. He died from cardiac arrhythmia consistent with an overdose of

Digitalis, complicated by oral ingestion of reactant foods and herbs."

"And you told me before those were elevated potassium from bananas, irregular heartbeat from black licorice, and increased digoxin from hawthorn berry and Siberian ginseng. Anything else?"

"Poisoning from foxglove plant. You know that's what *Digitalis* is derived from. Also, lily of the valley. That, in and of itself, is deadly."

"I do know. I can't for the life of me figure out where he got hold of those."

"Few people, outside of physicians, pharmacists, or herbalists like you know about them. I doubt very much a common layperson would be able to administer the herbs, much less identify them in nature."

"No, not unless they've been trained in wildcraft."

"Exactly. Are you thinking the Padilla woman?"

Tommie frowned. "I've talked to her, Sandy, and I truly believe she would never do that, even to a lowlife like Jimmy Clay."

"She had good reason, I'd say."

"What could ever be a good reason for murder?"

"Protection of your child or grandchild. Can you tell me you'd never kill someone who threatened or hurt Evie Kate, Karen Marie, or Kevin?"

"I might beat the living daylights out of somebody so badly they could die, like if I broke their nose into their skull with Kevin's childhood t-ball bat, but I couldn't plan

a killing."

"People never know what they'll do in that situation, Tommie. I can see it happening."

"But not premeditation, Sandy. Mrs. Padilla's not capable of carrying out the cold-blooded murder of three men, no matter how despicable they were."

"That's a good point you bring up. You know, all three of the victims died from the same combination of natural and pharmaceutical agents, and within minutes of one another. By my thinking, they had to ingest the toxins at roughly the same time."

"They were all sitting at the same table for a while."

"Tommie, you probably saw them consume it!"

"I probably did, but I didn't know what I was looking at. I've been going over and over the events. They all ate the same food. *We* all ate the same food, for that matter. Nobody else got sick, other than those who couldn't tolerate the heart burn from the spices and peppers or the overindulgence of alcohol."

"You just made me think of something else. Jimmy Clay's blood alcohol level was off the charts. But neither Larry Clay nor Dr. Frank had alcohol in their systems."

"Are you sure? I saw Larry Clay holding a beer."

"He smelled like booze, but he hadn't drunk any."

"Huh. That's odd. I remember seeing at least three bottles of beer at that table. Maybe the women had some."

"Maybe. But they've not ended up in my morgue, so I can't say."

"One last thing, Sandy. Did any of the men have preexisting conditions?"

"Yes. Dr. Frank had underlying heart problems. Ironic, isn't it, with him being a cardiologist? And he had chronic acid reflux. Apparently, he took antacids regularly, from what I could determine. His stomach contents revealed he ate a great deal of the spicy food and had taken an antacid tablet."

"Besides being toxic, foxglove and lily of the valley have an adverse reaction with antacids."

"You are entirely correct. That's why he ended up vomiting before he died, while Larry and Jimmy did not."

"Anything else, Sandy?"

"Jimmy Clay, in addition to being pretty well pickled, had an active disease that comes from, well, intimate contact, if you know what I mean."

"Ew. Hector Flores said Larry Clay gave him medication under the table for STDs."

"Hmm, yeah. That confirms what I found. His was antibiotic resistant. That comes from indiscriminate use of antibiotics without a prescribed regimen. So, Larry was supplying him off the books. Have you told Earl?"

"Not yet, but we have a date tonight, and I'll fill him in on our investigation."

Sandy snickered. "Getting to be pretty serious, cousin. Will you be Tommie Petry soon?"

"Neither of us wants to get married again, Sandy."

"Never say 'never,' Tommie. It's a good match, in

my opinion. He's one of my best friends, personally and professionally. You couldn't get a better man."

"Thank you, Yenta. I'll tell him you said so."

Chapter Twenty-One

FINBAR sat on a wrought iron bench outside Lassiter Law Offices. It was already getting hot at 9:30 in the morning, but he reveled in the heat. In Ireland, he would still be wearing a jacket and long pants instead of a t-shirt, jean shorts, and sandals. *I miss ye, Dublin, but I does love it here.* A scuffling sound behind him caught his attention.

"Good morning, Holmes. What brings you to this bench? Could it be the reading of Dr. Frank's will?"

Finbar turned with a smile. "Halloo, Detective. *Conas atá tú?* How are ye doing?"

Earl Petry sidled up beside Finbar and stretched out his long legs. "I'm peachy. Waiting for someone?"

"I am just enjoying this lovely weather. What makes ye think I'm waiting for anyone in particular?"

"You and Tommie are terrible liars. Who's the lucky person of interest? Male or female?"

Finbar pursed his thin lips and fluttered his lashes. "It could be a woman. Or it could be several women. I likes the ladies, ye know."

Earl scoffed. "Let me guess, Holmes. Elaine Frank? Simone Lorence? Katherine Clay?"

Finbar sat up. "Katherine Clay is named in Dr. Norman Frank's will?"

"Not that I'm aware. I believe she has other business concerning the benefits from her husband's insurance policy, as well as his will."

"Is that a fact? I do hope she's not been cut off without a penny. *Tsk tsk.* What's a body to do?"

"I hear she's not well pleased, if that's any indication. What do you know, and where is Tommie?"

"Thomasina slept badly, so she stayed home this morning. As for what we know, I'm sure she will fill ye in on yer date tonight. I don't know anything she doesn't."

Earl smiled and clapped Finbar on the back. "Be careful, you two. You understand I can't officially endorse your investigation, but I support you completely ... as long as you keep my girl safe from harm. I can't say how many lives that little kitty has left, but I want her to spend them all with me ... and you, to a certain extent."

Finbar winked. "I'm yer man, Detective. I'll protect her as ye would yerself." He noticed a couple exit the office and turn left toward the parking lot. "And now, m'thinks ye should make yerself scarce so I can do m'job. It appears the reading of the will has finished."

Earl rose from the bench and casually walked back toward the police station. Finbar kept his eyes on the door, hoping to catch one of the women leaving the office. He was rewarded with the sight of Simone Lorence and Katherine Clay coming down the steps. Their faces were splotchy, and their eye makeup seemed smudged. They appeared to be bickering as they hurried out toward a car on the same side of the street as the bench beneath the shade tree. Finbar sat quietly, unobtrusively observing them. He found he could hear their conversation clearly.

"I lived with him for seven years. Seven years! And he leaves his estate to an ex-wife?" Simone said.

"A 'faithful ex-wife' is what it said in the will," Katherine said.

Simone turned a savage face to her. "I know what the will said. Do you think I'm deaf? I was aware he was making changes, but I didn't think he had already done it. It was supposed to be for me. All of it! Seven years and nothing to show for it except the jewelry I already own!"

Katherine scoffed. "At least you got something. Larry left me nothing. Nothing! I was hoping he hadn't changed his insurance policy yet. At least, after the divorce, I would have been entitled to half of his assets."

"Why do you people say that? No, Katherine. You could *petition* for half of his assets, but you weren't *entitled* to them."

"But Florida law says ..."

"Florida law says there will be an 'equitable

distribution' of the marital assets and liabilities. Anyhow, it's a moot point since Larry died before the divorce was signed and filed. His final will and testimony clearly outline what you get. And you're right, it's nothing. Nothing for you. Nothing for your two sons from your first marriage. Did you know about that little girl?"

"I suspected. He wouldn't adopt *my* boys, but he wanted to get custody of *that* child. I was paying her mother to keep her from considering his bribes."

Simone derided her. "You're stupider than I thought. Don't you realize that can come back on you? People are going to find out she's his daughter."

"Maybe not. Maybe nobody noticed that cleft. He usually wore a beard that covered his chin."

"But not last Sunday. He shaved it off!"

I don't know why. He seemed to think the beard made him attractive to the younger women ..."

"... and girls."

Katherine grabbed Simone's arm. "You shut up, Simone. I bet you slept with him, too, didn't you?"

"No. The only man I shared with you was Jimmy."

"Jimmy. The cause of all our trouble—physically, emotionally, and monetarily. If he hadn't been blackmailing us and told Larry and Norman, I'd be the insurance beneficiary instead of that Mexican kid ..."

"... and I'd have Dr. Norman Frank's estate."

"Jimmy should have died a lot sooner."

"We should have made sure he did."

Katherine opened her car door and climbed in. Simone stood at the open door and leaned down toward her and spoke too softly for Finbar to hear. When she raised up, she spotted him from the corner of her vision.

"I am zo zorry, Katherine. I know you and Larry were zo happy togedzer. You will miss him terribly, *mon chéri.*" she said in a loud voice. "He was *ton amour*—your love. I will come to zee funeral, and we will cry togedzer over our lost loves. *Au revoir, mon ami.*" She crossed the street quickly, wiping invisible tears from her face.

Finbar pulled the corners of his mouth up into a smile. *Au revoir, indeed. 'Gotcha,' as they say in America.*

Chapter Twenty-Two

TOMMIE set her phone on the desk and reflected on her conversation with Jo Clay. She walked over to Finbar's unit, grabbed the legal pads, and brought them back to her office. She flipped a few pages and began writing.

SUSPECT INTERVIEW

JO(ANNE) CLAY – OWNER, THE CLAY PIGEON

INTERVIEWED: on phone

MOTIVE #1: (Jimmy Clay) – Anger, Coverup – stalked, assaulted her; threatened to tell Santino depraved lies

MOTIVE #2: (Larry Clay) – none apparent

MOTIVE #3: (Norman Frank) – none apparent

ALIBI #1: no access to *Digitalis*

ALIBI #2: no access to *Digitalis*

ALIBI #3: no access to *Digitalis*

LIES: Didn't know Lara was raped by Jimmy

TRUTHS: prepared Jo's Red Salsa and Elly's layered dip; helped Dearci make ceramic bowls

IMPLICATES: Gertrudis, Lara

GOSSIP & HEARSAY: Jimmy showed too much interest in teenage Lara Padilla; Gertrudis vowed to kill whoever raped Lara; Lara hated Jimmy

QUESTIONS: Did she know Dearci's real father?

OBSERVATIONS: seems sincere

UNCOVERED FACTS: slashed Jimmy's arm with knife once when he hit her

Since Finbar had not filled out the next suspect interview, Tommie completed it.

SANTINO ALVAREZ – OWNER, SANTINO'S SHOE SHOP, LEO'S LEATHER GOODS

INTERVIEWED: by Earl at shop

MOTIVE #1: (Jimmy Clay) – Anger, Revenge – stalked, assaulted Jo; spread rumors about her

MOTIVE #2: (Larry Clay) – none apparent

MOTIVE #3: (Norman Frank) – none apparent

ALIBI #1: no access to *Digitalis*; only hit once

ALIBI #2: no access to *Digitalis*; fighting Jimmy

ALIBI #3: no access to *Digitalis;* fighting Jimmy

LIES: Pulled his punch to be less lethal

TRUTHS: prepared beef jerky sold by Don/Henry. Warned Jimmy to stay away from Jo. Saw Jimmy follow Jo. Defended Jo from Jimmy's advances.

IMPLICATES: self

GOSSIP & HEARSAY: Jimmy spread malicious rumors about Jo

QUESTIONS: Did he seek out Jimmy to fight with?

OBSERVATIONS: afraid of arrest or deportation

UNCOVERED FACTS: Santino & Leo street fighters in Mexico. Known for one-punch knockouts. Killed opponent by accident.

Tommie skipped through the pages to fill in the blanks for other suspects.

ELAINE FRANK – OWNER, FLORIBUNDA REAL PROPERTIES

INTERVIEWED: Tommie, in shop

MOTIVE #1: (Jimmy Clay) – none apparent

MOTIVE #2: (Larry Clay) – none apparent

MOTIVE #3: (Norman Frank) – Greed, Revenge, Coverup – 2nd husband paying "alimony" (hush money to keep quiet about death of Salvador Padilla); divorced her for Simone; afraid he would cut her off soon because of Simone

ALIBI #1: no access to *Digitalis*

ALIBI #2: no access to *Digitalis*

ALIBI #3: no access to *Digitalis*

LIES: none known

TRUTHS: sold Jo's Red Salsa and Elly's layered dip; kept alimony check but donated cash each month

IMPLICATES: self, Gertrudis, Lara

GOSSIP & HEARSAY: Larry Clay was Dearci's father; Dr. Frank and Larry Clay overprescribed

medications for money; Larry gave Jimmy free medicine for STDs

QUESTIONS: Is she in Dr. Frank's will?

OBSERVATIONS: remorseful

UNCOVERED FACTS: Received $7,500 month cash from Dr. Frank, gave it to charity, did not report to IRS; deposited $1,500 month into Padilla account (guilt, restitution).

Tommie looked over the entries, searching for patterns in motives and checking alibis. The most striking commonalities she found were the statements "no access to *Digitalis*" and two names: Gertrudis and Lara Padilla.

Chapter Twenty-Three

EARL picked Tommie up outside Caife Caife Holmes at 7:00 that evening, as was the standing routine for their Wednesday night dinner dates. He noticed she carried a canvas tote bag which was emblazoned with a logo and the words "Florida Teacher Award."

"Is this a new fashion statement, darlin', or did Holmes give you takeout food?" he said with a smirk.

Tommie rolled her eyes. "No, this is research we've compiled for our investigation. I thought you and I might go over it after dinner."

Earl scowled. "Does that mean no dessert?"

She grinned. "Not necessarily. But maybe we can delay dessert a little bit. I really need some help correlating all this information, and you're the best detective I know, outside of Finbar and myself."

He planted a kiss on her cheek. "OK. I've got an idea, though. Why don't we take our dinner on The Fallen Oak's patio? It's not too hot outside, and there should be fewer people around to hear us. I'm not against shop talk at dinner. I *am* against shop talk interfering with dessert."

"Deal. Full disclosure? Full sharing of info?"

"Yup. Just so long as ..."

"... dessert."

Earl grinned and led Tommie to a secluded table in the corner of the restaurant's screened-in patio. Overhead ceiling fans with imitation bamboo paddles circulated air, and several strings of round lightbulbs provided ample illumination without being glaring. There was only one other table occupied, and it was on the opposite side of the porch. Earl pulled out Tommie's chair and directed the server to bring ice water for her and a cold beer for himself. While they waited for their drinks and their usual food order, Earl caught Tommie's feet between his beneath the table and reached forward to take her hand. They had fallen into this easy habit during the many weeks in which their relationship progressed.

"Hello, my love. I've missed you this week."

"And I've missed you, too, although I've been so busy with this dang case."

"Do you have it narrowed down to any suspects yet?" he asked her.

"Yes, and no. We've basically got nine possible suspects, but not all of them have motive or means for all

three deaths. That's what's got us stumped."

"Who's on your list?"

"Gertrudis and Lara Padilla, Katherine Clay, Simone Lorence, Hector Flores, Elaine Frank, Santino Alvarez, Jo Clay, and possibly Susan Clay."

Earl took a healthy swig from his cold mug of beer, then wiped foam from his white mustache.

"Elaine and Susan? Really? They're ex-wives and have been for a number of years. I'm not inclined to think of either woman, but I'm sure you have reason. And Santino? Sandy said the punch didn't kill Jimmy Clay, and Santino was nowhere near the other two men. We are looking into Hector Flores because of his pharmacy connection with the *Digitalis* and Mrs. Padilla because of the toxic herbs and the fact that Dr. Frank was responsible for her husband's death. I'm not so sure about the daughter. The victims' wife and girlfriend haven't yet been ruled out."

"Do you have any other suspects we've missed, Earl? We've talked with the other vendors, but we don't believe any of them are viable."

"No, not really. Show me what you've got."

Tommie reached into her bag and withdrew the colored radial graphs and flow chart. Earl studied them and smiled appreciatively.

"Wow. You've done some damn good work, darlin'. I wish I had you on the payroll. Can I keep these?"

"Yep. I have them on my computer. Do you see what I mean about how elusive this case is? It's hard to pin

any one person down … except for Gertrudis. I honestly can't believe she would do this, not to mention I don't know how she'd get her hands on *Digitalis*." Tommie abruptly brought her hand to her mouth. Her eyes widened, and she stared at Earl with a stricken look. "Oh no, Earl!"

"What is it, Tommie? What's the matter?"

"I just realized something. Salvador Padilla had heart failure. Dr. Frank prescribed *Digitalis* for him. Larry Clay filled the prescription."

"What happened to it after Mr. Padilla died? Prescription medications are supposed to be disposed of after the patient is dead."

"What if she didn't throw it away? That gives her access to it to use as a murder weapon, and …"

"And the daughter would have access to it, too."

Tommie's eyes filled with tears.

"Darlin'?"

"I don't want it to be them, Earl. I don't."

"Maybe not, Tommie. Maybe not. But we have to follow up on it to be certain. Damnit. I was leaning toward Katherine and Simone."

"Yeah, so is Finbar after he overheard their conversation this morning."

"Uh huh. Fill me in on that."

"He hid out on a nearby bench, and they didn't notice him listening. They basically said they were both cut out of the wills. Dr. Frank left his estate to Elaine. Larry left his possessions to other family members, but not to

Katherine. Apparently, Simone and Katherine both slept with Jimmy Clay. Not only was he blackmailing them, he went ahead and told his brother and Dr. Frank about it! And … Finbar said Simone didn't have a French accent."

Earl cut into his rib-eye steak. "I thought she sounded kinda fake. I wonder if she kept up the ruse with her boyfriend all those years. Interesting."

"Elaine said she used it to snag Dr. Frank. He was pretty taken with her as a little French *coquette.*"

"Yuck. She never appealed to me. Tommie, why do you think Elaine got his estate after all this time?"

She avoided his gaze. "She, uh, she knew about the malpractice death of Mr. Padilla and kept quiet."

Earl chewed his food and established eye contact.

Tommie sipped her water and blinked back at him innocently. "What?"

"What else?"

She blew out a sigh. "He paid her under the table to keep the secret … and she didn't report it to the IRS."

Earl wiped his mouth. "I'm not investigating tax matters. I'm interested in the murders."

Tommie nodded. "OK. That makes me feel a little better. There's more to her story that I'll tell you later."

"All right. What do you have on Susan?"

"Nothing, except Larry ran around on her and divorced her for Katherine, then he quit paying alimony."

"I can't see that as a reason for murder."

"And Larry had an appetite for young girls."

"I heard about that, but I couldn't confirm it."

"Oh, wait! I didn't tell you ... Larry Clay's insurance beneficiary was a child."

"Not one of Katherine's children?"

"No. A little Mexican girl."

"Dearcilla Padilla."

"That's the one."

"I thought Jimmy Clay fathered her. There was talk he assaulted Lara as a teenager, but we couldn't do anything because she wouldn't come forward about the incident."

"He did assault her, but she was seduced beforehand by Larry Clay. There's no way to determine, without a DNA test, which one really fathered Dearci."

Earl sat still. His nostrils flared, and a vein throbbed in his temple as he tightly clenched his jaw. Tommie stabbed a forkful of roast chicken and slowly brought it to her mouth.

"I've never known three men who were more deserving of killing," Earl said, once he composed himself.

"Um. Jo stabbed Jimmy one time when he hit her."

"Good for her. What else have you got?"

"Most of the alibis for the suspects come down to no access to *Digitalis*. But, in the case of Gertrudis and Lara, that's not true anymore."

"Yup. And it's also the case for Simone and Katherine, if you think about it. One lived with a cardiologist, and the other lived with a pharmacist."

"Oh my, Earl. You're right! We completely

overlooked that. Hector Flores, of course, is a pharmacist. And, if I'm not mistaken, I think that will take Santino, Elaine, and Susan off the hook."

"Quite possibly." Earl looked at her plate. "Are you done with dinner?"

Tommie frowned. She had only eaten about half of her meal, and he still have a large portion of steak left. "Uh, I guess so, if you are."

"No, I'm not, but I'm tired of sitting here." He signaled the server. "Bring the check, please, and we'll take a couple of doggie bags."

"Would you care for dessert, sir?" the waiter asked.

Earl winked at Tommie. "No, thanks. We'll have our dessert at home."

Chapter Twenty-Four

FINBAR arrived early the following morning at the Floribunda Police Department after receiving a call from a desperate Leo Alvarez. Santino had been arrested for assault with a deadly weapon—the weapon being his fists. After paying Santino's bail, Finbar brought the two men back to his duplex where he set about preparing a hearty breakfast. Tommie entered the kitchen at 8:00 as usual and was surprised to see the additional guests at the table.

"Leo! Santino! This is a surprise." She looked from one to the other. "What's wrong? Why are you here?"

"There's been a miscarriage of justice, missus, involving Santino's use of deadly force," Finbar explained.

"What? That's ridiculous. Everybody saw that he only hit the man once. Even Sandy said he didn't kill him with that punch."

"That is true, *señora,* but I have a record back in Mexico. I am forbidden to fight because of the harm I have caused," Santino said.

"And Earl arrested you?" Her voice was shrill.

"No, no. He did not. It was another officer I do not know. *El detective* was the one who spoke to the judge on my behalf."

"*Sí.* It has been called a mistake, but we are afraid of being sent back. We have not yet taken our citizenship tests. We may have to return to Mexico," Leo said.

"Rubbish," Finbar called from the stove. "Ye'll not be deported whilst I have anything to say of it. I'll be yer advocate, lads."

"Finbar, you're not an American citizen either. I'm sure Earl can do something about this. Just let me give him a call." Tommie walked into the other room, cellphone already up to her ear, and spoke in hushed tones. When she returned, she took a seat at the table and smiled. "Never you worry. Earl is already petitioning on your behalf. Let's eat. I'm starved."

"Right away, yer majesty," Finbar said, depositing serving plates on the table laden with scrambled eggs, bacon rashers, cherry tomatoes, sliced onions, pork 'n' beans, brown bread, and Wexford cheese. "Mind the beans, lads. Missus Thomasina doesn't like the aftereffects overmuch."

The Alvarez brothers bowed their heads and silently blessed their food before helping themselves to the feast. Not to be outdone, Finbar made the sign of the cross.

Tommie lifted her eyebrows and refrained from commenting as she observed the rituals.

"Lads," Finbar said, "d'you think ye might be of help to us in our task to bring the murderer to bear?"

"We may not know much to help, *señor,* but we will try," Leo said.

"Lovely. We've spoken with the people from the Greenleaf community, but I find them reluctant to provide many details. What can ye tell me about Hector Flores?"

"He is a fine man. He is hardworking and very smart. He has a degree from a college. Carmine has the arthritis very bad. She takes much medicine, but I think she suffers pain all the time," Santino said.

"Hector has been working at the Rx-All many years, but *Señor* Beadwell gives the advancement to *Señor* Clay instead of Hector. He must work another job to pay for medicine for *Señora* Flores," Leo said.

"Other than Larry Clay and Tom Beadwell, I guess, does Hector have any enemies?" Tommie asked.

"No. The doctor, maybe. He encouraged the advancement of *Señor* Clay," Santino admitted.

"What about Jimmy Clay?" Finbar asked.

Santino and Leo glowered and shrugged.

"He was liked by nobody. Everyone will tell you he was a bad man," Leo said.

"Have ye ever heard Mr. Flores speak of the victims in a disparaging manner?" Finbar asked.

"Disparaging? You mean saying a bad thing?" Leo

cut his eyes at Santino. "I heard him say things of all those men, but I think he meant no harm."

Santino dropped his fork in his plate and stared at his brother. Leo avoided his eyes and continued eating.

"Like what, Leo? We only want to get to the truth. We don't want to get you or Santino or Hector into trouble," Tommie said, keeping an eye on Santino.

Leo hung his head. "He says they are not worth breathing the air. He says that the world would be a better place without them. He says, if he could, he would give them a taste of their own medicine."

Finbar and Tommie stopped eating and sat quietly as Leo and Santino had a terse exchange in Spanish. After a few moments, Santino excused himself from the table and strode outside into the back yard, followed by the dogs.

Leo raised his chin. "Santino thinks I should say nothing, but I must say the truth. Hector Flores had reason to kill those men. Gertrudis Padilla had reason to kill those men. Lara Padilla had reason to kill those men. Santino, Jo, I, or my Elly had reason to kill those men. But I have prayed for guidance, and my heart tells me that whoever did kill those men was filled with evil. And I believe, in my heart, the people you suspect are filled with good. The deaths of these men? It had to be, but somebody else did it."

Santino shuffled back into the kitchen, the three dogs on his heels. "I am sorry for my temper. I have no excuse except I am afraid. *Mi hermano* is more a man than I. He has no fear of saying the truth."

"I've another truth for ye, lad. Yer plate is still set at m'table, and yer always welcome as m'guest. Come and sit. I knows ye don't drink coffee, but missus Thomasina has a fine herbal tea hot in the kettle that I'm sure ye will like," Finbar said, gesturing to the empty chair.

Santino sat down, and the four of them finished breakfast with more congenial conversation. Afterward, Holmes dropped the Alvarez brothers off at their shops before going to Caife Caife Holmes.

Tommie drove her own car and parked, then she walked across the asphalt lot to The Clay Pigeon. When she stuck her head in the back door, she was pleased to see Lara Padilla there with Dearci. The little girl ran to Tommie and gave her a hug before returning to a long table filled with pottery in various stages of completion.

"Hi, Tommie," Jo called. "Come join us. We're making mugs for your shop."

Tommie sat down beside Dearci and inspected the project the child was working on. The greenware mugs were pre-made, but Dearci was busy decorating them. She carefully painted over tiny flowers, seeds, and leaves which had been pressed into the clay.

"Wow. So pretty. And these will be for me? I'm honored. How do you make them?" Tommie asked.

Dearci held up a mug that was a dark grey color next to one that was chalky white. "First we put the pretty things in the greenware using slip. That's watery clay to hold them in better. Then Miss Jo fires them in the kiln.

And that makes them white. Oh, I forgot what it's called."

"Bisque," Jo said.

Dearci giggled. "Yeah, like biscuit but different. After it turns white, I paint over the whole thing with glaze." She held up a mug that was covered with a cloudy, translucent mixture over chopped up violet-colored flowers. "This one is gonna be purple, but it doesn't look like it until it cooks in the kiln again. And it'll be shiny, too, on top of the pretty decorations."

"That's fascinating, Dearci. You really know what you're doing," Tommie said.

"Miss Jo is a good teacher."

"Where did you get all the flowers and seeds?"

"I find them on the ground or in the woods by my house. My *abuela* has pretty flowers in her garden. I pick the berries and save them in a box. They get dried up and stick in the ceramics better that way. Sometimes, Mama lets me use her spices. Did you know there's one shaped like a star? I put that on one of your mugs with a yellow glaze."

"It's called star anise. It smells good, too."

"Yeah. I put some of those clove things and some orange flowers on another mug. I covered it with orange glaze. It'll look cool."

"I love all the different colors."

"I made a pink one with white flowers, and a blue one with dried blueberries, and a red one with paper-eeka."

"Paper-eeka? I'm not familiar with that."

"Paprika," Jo said with a smile. "Dearci, pay

attention to what you're doing, honey. Make sure the glaze completely covers the bisqueware. If you don't, there'll be unglazed spots that will soak up liquid. Miss Tommie doesn't want tea that tastes like paprika or onions."

"Onion tea!" Dearci laughed aloud and focused on her painting. Tommie walked over to Lara while Jo supervised the little girl's work.

"Hi, Lara. She really is quite the artist."

Lara smiled. "Yes, she loves it. Maybe she can make an occupation of it one day, unless my mother has her way and makes her into another herbalist."

"I understand she's teaching Dearci the practice."

"She has been since the child was able to hold a pair of blunt scissors. 'Cut here. Take the flowers gently. Don't use that leaf. Hang them upside down to dry.' Dearci even has her own herbal collection kit that my mother made for her. She keeps her scissors and gloves in it with a bunch of paper sacks for storing her finds."

"I think that's wonderful. Maybe she can do both. She can be an herbalist that makes her own containers."

Lara shrugged. "Could be."

"Lara, I wanted to ask you about Sunday. I saw Jimmy Clay say something to Dearci, and it made you angry. Can you tell me what he said?"

Lara looked at her daughter, then lowered her voice to a whisper. "You know I had Dearci when I was 16. And I'm not proud of it, but there was a man I cared about who was much older. He quit seeing me after we—you know.

And Jimmy Clay came along and said the man gave him permission to have me, as if I was a dog he was giving away. I tried to fight him off, but he beat me up and forced me."

"Lara, I'm so sorry that happened to you."

"Yeah, well. He said nobody would believe me if I reported him, so I kept quiet. My mother knew, though, because she nursed my cuts and bruises. I got pregnant, and Jimmy didn't bother me again, but the other man said he never told Jimmy he could have me, and he said he wanted my baby. But, Ms. Watson, that's *my* baby, and nobody else can have her—especially those two men."

"I completely understand. So, what did Jimmy say to Dearci that distressed you?"

"She was giving out salsa in those little bowls she made. She even added extra cilantro and garnishes for some of the people she liked until I told her it would change the flavor. Anyway, he was harassing Jo, and Dearci was standing there. He looked at her and said, 'Where did you get them dimples and dark blue eyes?' And Dearci said, 'My daddy gave them to me.' Then he put his filthy hand on my daughter's face! I could've killed him right there, but I didn't. I pulled my baby away and kept her behind the table from then on out." Lara's eyes, instead of being filled with tears, blazed with passion.

"You're a strong woman, Lara Padilla. I admire your protective instinct for your child. In your position, I think I would feel exactly the same way. I'm going to ask you straight out. Did you kill him?"

Lara didn't flinch or blink. "No. I did not kill him. I did not kill his brother, and I did not kill that doctor who murdered my father."

"Thank you, Lara. I believe you." Tommie smiled, but Lara didn't return the smile.

"I didn't kill them, but make no mistake about it, Ms. Watson. Where my daughter is concerned, I'm entirely capable of violence."

Chapter Twenty-Five

TOMMIE AND FINBAR spent Friday morning preparing for Finbar's Saturday night grand re-launch of the Caife Caife Holmes dinner demonstrations and Tommie's Sunday Mother's Day Tea Party. Though their friends from Floribunda and Riverton had banded together to restore the two shops after Louanne Weller tried to burn them up, Finbar had yet to replenish his pantry supplies. Since his event occurred first, he and Tommie concentrated on getting his food items ready.

Finbar planned to hold a Mexican themed cooking demonstration. The menu included *Tamale Pie, Mexican Flan,* and *Mexican Coffee.* While Finbar named off the ingredients, Tommie assembled them.

"For the dry ingredients, I need cornmeal and flour," he said.

"Got it." Tommie put the respective containers on his counter.

"I shall require honey, olive oil, tinned creamed corn, and tinned black olives. For the herbs, I need chili powder, garlic, cilantro, salt, and pepper."

"I've got them all here on this baking dish. Next?"

"Refrigerated items. Six eggs, buttermilk, green onion, ground beef, cheddar jack cheese, sour cream, and the *Easy Enchilada Sauce* you made for the celebration."

"All righty. Top shelf, first refrigerator."

"Lovely. That takes care of the *Tamale Pie*. Now, for the *Mexican Flan*. I need three tins of evaporated milk, three tins of sweetened condensed milk, sugar, and vanilla. For the refrigerator, 18 eggs and three packages cream cheese. And set out the aluminum foil, please."

"OK. All done, plus the a-lu-min-i-um foil."

"Thomasina, shall I make fun of yer dialect?"

She snickered. "Ha, couldn't resist. What's next?"

"For the *Mexican Coffee*, could you set the dark roast coffee beans over next to the grinder, please? Yes. And check the other refrigerator. I should have heavy cream and whole milk in there. I shall also need cinnamon, dark brown sugar, an orange, vanilla, and the semisweet dark chocolate."

"It's all ready, Finbar. It even makes me want to drink coffee, sorta."

"As you say, missus. I'll believe it when I sees it. Shall we try to tackle yer sandwich makings? I have to say I think ye may be overdoing it, but, sure, ye knows what ye

likes to do."

The two of them went through the connecting door to Watson's Reme-Teas and portioned out the ingredients for the 12 different tea sandwiches she would serve on Sunday. Once divided, they each took a different sandwich filling to prepare. Together, they worked like a well-oiled machine.

Finbar combined cream cheese, black olives, and pepperoni slices and sealed them in a lidded container that read *"bat sandwich 1."* Then, he mixed marshmallow fluff and Nutella brand spread in the container that read *"bat sandwich 2."* He stacked the containers in the refrigerator.

Tommie chopped boiled eggs and mixed them with yogurt, pickle relish, and paprika for *"swan sandwich 1."* Then, she coarsely chopped chicken breasts and added mayonnaise and grapes for *"swan sandwich 2."*

Finbar prepared the fillings for the two *"cow sandwiches"* and the two *"kangaroo sandwiches,"* while Tommie mixed up the *"seal sandwiches"* and the *"llama sandwiches."* After all the mixed fillings had been prepared and placed in their respective containers inside the refrigerators, Finbar and Tommie separated the different breads, cut them into small individual portions, and stored them inside sealed plastic bags in the pantry.

"I never would have believed it, missus. All them sandwich types. Yer mammies and babbies will love them," Finbar said as he washed and dried his hands by the sink. "I made up some extra of m'special *Matcha Shortbread*

Biscuits ye can have for yer Saturday story time. Don't let me forget to give them to ye."

"Thanks! I'll call them cookies, if it's all the same to you. Southerners have a different expectation of the word biscuit." She winked. "Seriously, Finbar, I really couldn't have done all this without your help. And look! I still have a half hour to spare before I open up. Let's have a cup of tea and some *Mama Llama Munchie Mix.*"

Tommie scooped out a portion of the mix with a large mug and placed it on a table, along with two of the tiny salsa bowls. While she went to steep the tea, Finbar examined the ceramicware.

"Ye say Dearcilla made the bowls and this mug? She's got a talent. They're quite lovely. D'you know what kinds of flowers and whatnot she's put on them?"

Tommie brought the tea to the table and picked up the mug. "That would be chamomile—the white flowers with yellow centers. The oval shaped ones are lavender. She's pressed some peppermint leaves into the sides, too. Ah ha! She told me she liked cloves. See them stuck here and there between the leaves?"

"Brilliant. What's on the salsa bowls?"

"Hmm. From the shape of it, I believe that glossy green leaf across the bottom of the bowl is *Allium ursinum,* also called Ramsons garlic. The plant has white flowers. Looks like Dearci chopped them up and sprinkled them on the leaf. The chopped pinky-purple flowers appear to be Oxalis, known as pink wood sorrel."

"Are they non-toxic on food containers?"

"Well, yes. In this small of an amount there would be no harm. Any herb or plant consumed in large quantities could potentially be toxic. Besides, she was at Jo's this morning making me some mugs. Jo made sure she covered the entire surface with glaze so there's no chance of any contact with the plants embedded in the bowls and mugs."

"Well, dear, it's nearly time for ye to open yer shop. I'll be getting on over to mine. See you at half five to help me serve the coffee and biscuit-cookies."

Finbar disappeared through the connecting door. Tommie quickly put away the mug and bowls, spritzed the table with an alcohol and peroxide mixture, and wiped it clean. Then, she put a smile on her face, turned her sign from CLOSED to OPEN, and happily welcomed her waiting lunch customers.

Chapter Twenty-Six

TOMMIE was delighted with the turnout for her story time event. Despite the gruesome outcome of the *Cinco de Mayo* celebration the previous weekend, Watson's Reme-Teas was filled with children and parents anxious to hear *Is Your Mama a Llama?* read in both English and Spanish and curious to try the treats she had laid out.

Santino and Leo Alvarez appeared a bit hesitant at first, afraid of the reception they might receive from those who had witnessed Santino knock out Jimmy Clay. Their trepidation was short-lived, however, as soon as their fiancés began interacting with the patrons. Jo Clay was much loved in the town of Floribunda for providing a creative outlet for kids of all ages. Elly James, with her head full of blond ringlets, bright blue eyes, and infectious smile, was what Tommie referred to as "a child magnet." The

youngest ones, especially, were drawn to her.

Tommie was happy to see Dearcilla Padilla. She had been brought to the shop by Carmine Flores. Gertrudis and Lara were conspicuously absent.

"Hi, Carmine. I see you have Dearci with you. Is Lara working today?" Tommie said.

"She was unable to come."

"Is she sick?"

Carmine winced. "No. She is well enough."

Tommie leaned closer. "Carmine? What's wrong? Are you in pain?"

Carmine turned slightly and nodded. Tommie noticed her eyes were red rimmed, there were furrows in her brow, and her lips twitched slightly.

Tommie laid her hand softly on the woman's shoulder. "Let me bring you something that might help."

Carmine reached up and grasped Tommie's hand. "I can manage the physical pain. It is the emotional pain that afflicts me." She slowly got to her feet and moved to the edge of the room, away from listening ears, taking Tommie with her.

"Carmine? What is it?"

"They have taken Lara, Gertrudis, and my Hector to the police station for more questioning. Hector believes they may be charged as conspirators for last week's deaths."

"But why?"

"They all had reasons to kill those men."

"Lots of people had reasons, but that doesn't make

them murderers."

"And they all had the means to get *Digitalis*. Yes, Ms. Watson, I know that's what led to their deaths."

"How did you find out?"

Carmine uttered a weak laugh. "Tommie Watson, you're not the only detective in the world. You forget, I have a college education and a teaching degree, and I know how to conduct an internet search."

Tommie's face colored. "I didn't mean to imply anything. I just wondered."

"Don't worry. I understand what you meant. Listen, my Hector is the most attentive and loving man I've ever met. My disease is debilitating, and the medication is expensive. He works two jobs, and I try to accept every substitute teaching assignment I can, even when all I want to do is lie in bed. We struggle to make our monthly bills."

"I'm so sorry. I can't help your financial situation, but I can prepare something to ease your pain and the inflammation, and I won't even charge you."

Carmine smiled and patted Tommie's hand. "You are a dear woman. Hector says you have a healing gift. But he also has a gift, and he is able to make compounds and creams that stave off the pain a great deal. Larry Clay's promotion hurt us, and it may seem that the only way Hector could advance was for Larry to be out of the way, but he has just gotten a raise at Winn-Dixie, and he believes they may promote him before long."

"What can I do to help, then?"

"Speak to your boyfriend. Tell him to look further at who else might have been able to get *Digitalis*. Consider Gertrudis, Lara, and Hector as people and not just suspects. They had the means, and you could even say they had motives, but none of them would risk committing murder. To do so would mean risking their families. I ask you, is revenge or greed or even desperation worth the loss of those for whom you care the most?"

Carmine Flores made her way back to her chair just in time for Dearci to bring punch and treats for them to share. The little girl blew a kiss to Tommie from across the room, and it was like a dagger in Tommie's heart.

Chapter Twenty-Seven

FINBAR was in his element that night at the re-launch of his reservations-only cooking demonstration. Not only were the guests there to eat and learn to prepare the foods on his menu, but they were also there to celebrate the upcoming marriages of Santino, Jo, Leo, and Elly. All 20 seats were filled. In attendance were the Fab Four—Elaine, Susan, Don, and Henry—who were the unofficial organizers of the engagement dinner. Other attendees included Tina Brass, Joan Carrol, and Annie Lang (the Songbirds), Craig and Maggie Kohl and Terry Jackson (the Riverton friends), León and Letitia Luz, Jorge and Soledad Fuentes (Greenfield residents), Levi Muller, and Aubrey Rush. Tommie stuck to her stool behind the counter, and Finbar swept back and forth mixing, stirring, tasting, and talking.

By all accounts, it should have been a joyous

occasion, but Tommie was riddled with guilt about the apprehension of Gertrudis, Lara, and Hector. She lamented silently with a fake smile pasted on her face. *I've got to make this right, but I'm lost. Bogged down with the details.*

Somehow, she made it through the evening without putting a damper on the festivities, but when she got home, the first thing she did was call her son, Kevin.

"Hey, Mom. How was Finbar's re-launch?"

"Oh, it was good, honey."

"Glad to hear it, but why do you sound like it wasn't so good?"

"This case is getting to me. I can't make sense of it, and it looks like some good people may be blamed. I can't help thinking I'm missing something essential."

"Maybe I can give you a fresh viewpoint. Want to share your thoughts with me?

Tommie was relieved. "Yes! Thank you, son."

"Cool. Start at the beginning. Tell me who died and how, then tell me each suspect and why you think they might have done it."

For the next half hour, she went over the case files with Kevin, filling him in on motives, alibis, truths, lies, gossip, and observations about each suspect and material witness. He listened quietly, interjecting here and there for clarification of minor details and major occurrences.

Tommie left nothing out. Though Kevin was only 33, he had an amazing insight into people and their motivations. Tommie thought perhaps it was because of his

experience as a restaurant manager on Sugar Sand Beach—
a bustling melting pot of divergent personalities of all ages.
Add to that his childhood growing up in the small town of
Riverton, and he had a perspective unlike hers and Finbar's.

"Yowzer. That's a lot to take in, Mom. Sounds like
your victims deserved their fates. Greed, malpractice,
wrongful death, blackmail, pedophilia, rape, extortion,
adultery, intimidation. I don't know why somebody didn't
bump them off long before now," Kevin said.

"Yep. Me, too. What really sticks out to you, son?"

"First off, I agree with the substitute teacher. Why
risk being taken away from your family just to get revenge?"

"Exactly. What else?"

"I'm a little concerned about your friend not
reporting that money to the IRS. She's going to have to
make arrangements to pay that back. Maybe she can sell
that estate she inherited."

"Good point. I'll mention it to her."

"Another thing, Mom. You know about the
principle of Occam's razor, don't you?"

"The simplest solution is usually the best one."

"Yeah. Apply that principle. What's the simplest
solution for each murder? Or even, what's the simplest
solution for all the murders as one murder? Like Finbar
says, it all comes down to motive. Who has the best motive,
not for killing *each* man, but for killing *all three* men? Does
that help?"

"It actually does, Kevin. It's making me shift my

focus. A change of paradigm. One murder as opposed to three separate individual murders."

"Maybe. But let me put another spin on things. I know y'all usually dissect yourselves as suspects. Have you done the same with your victims?"

"You mean, think of them as suspects?"

"Yeah. Why not? Do some more digging into victimology. See what turns up that *made* them victims. Then apply the same Occam's razor principle. The simplest solution is usually the right one."

"Oh my gosh. How did I raise such a genius? I love you, sweetie, but I've got to go. Got three murders to solve."

"Love you, too, Mom. The game's afoot . . . again."

Chapter Twenty-Eight

FINBAR took the case files Tommie had left on his kitchen table to his easy chair. Because it was Sunday, the day of her Mother's Day Tea Party, she ate breakfast hurriedly and then went on to her shop to be sure everything was in order. She had refused his offer to help her construct her sandwiches, preferring to do them herself to divert her attention from the investigation. She told him about her conversation with Kevin that led her to stay up late compiling information about the victims.

Finbar reached into the drawer of his end table, withdrew his deep bowled pipe, and hung it on his lower lip. *Let's see what ye have here, missus.* He propped his feet up on the ottoman and began looking over the notes.

VICTIM I: JIMMY CLAY

Finbar skimmed the initial information, which included description and cause of death, and went straight

to the list of facts and motives compiled by Tommie.

<u>WHY WAS JIMMY CLAY A TARGET FOR MURDER?</u>

1. GERTRUDIS—raped Lara, thought he was Dearci's father, harassed Lara, would have told Dearci *(revenge, protection)*
2. KATHERINE—slept with her, blackmailed, told Larry *(revenge, coverup)*
3. SIMONE—slept with her, blackmailed, told Dr. Frank *(revenge, coverup)*
4. LARA—raped her, stalked her, bothered Dearci *(revenge, protection)*
5. HECTOR—got free meds for STDs from Larry *(??)*
6. ELAINE—knew about $$? *(coverup?)*
7. JO—beat/abused her, stalked her, spread rumors *(revenge)*
8. SANTINO—threatened fiancé, spread nasty rumors *(protection)*
9. SUSAN—*(??)*
10. LARRY CLAY—slept with Katherine, blackmailed, claimed to be Dearci's father, knew Larry liked young girls *(revenge, protection, coverup)*
11. DR. NORMAN FRANK—slept with Simone, blackmailed, knew about malpractice death, knew about medication scam *(revenge, protection, coverup)*

Finbar reread the last two suspects on the list. *Larry*

Clay and Dr. Norman Frank? Interesting, Thomasina. He turned to the next page.

VICTIM 2: LARRY CLAY

<u>WHY WAS LARRY CLAY A TARGET FOR MURDER?</u>

1. GERTRUDIS—slept with 16 y.o. Lara, Dearci's father, bribing her to get custody of Dearci, dispensed medicine that caused Salvador's death *(revenge, protection)*
2. KATHERINE—was Dearci's father, bribing Lara for custody of Dearci, overlooked her sons, was divorcing her because of affair with Jimmy, changing will *(revenge, greed, coverup)*
3. SIMONE—knew she slept with Jimmy, confirmed it to Dr. Frank *(revenge, greed)*
4. LARA—seduced her at age 16, fathered Dearci, trying to get custody of Dearci *(revenge, protection)*
5. HECTOR—overruled his catch of incorrect medication, blamed him for discrepancies in books, secured promotion over him, made him have to find 2ⁿᵈ job, paid too much attention to young girls, *(revenge, protection)*
6. ELAINE—ran around on sister Susan, knew he liked young girls, involved in malpractice death and incorrect prescriptions, knew about Simone *(protection, revenge)*
7. JO—*(??)*
8. SANTINO—*(??)*

9. SUSAN—ran around on her, liked young girls, fathered a child, stopped paying alimony *(revenge)*

10. JIMMY CLAY—knew he slept with Katherine, knew he claimed to be Dearci's father, knew he was being blackmailed (malpractice death, seducing young girls, giving STD meds for free), threatened to tell *(revenge, coverup)*

11. DR. NORMAN FRANK—knew about malpractice death, was part of medication scam, knew he pressured Tom Beadwell for the promotion *(coverup)*

Finbar turned to the next page and continued reading her list.

VICTIM 3: DR. NORMAN FRANK

<u>WHY WAS DR. FRANK A TARGET FOR MURDER?</u>

1. GERTRUDIS—caused husband Salvador's death with improper treatment and incorrect medication prescription, acquitted of malpractice w/no settlement *(revenge)*

2. KATHERINE—knew she slept with Jimmy, was changing will to cut her best friend out, was going to tell Larry of her affair *(revenge, greed, coverup)*

3. SIMONE—knew she slept with Jimmy, was changing will to cut her out *(revenge, greed)*

4. LARA—caused father's death with improper treatment and incorrect medication

prescription, acquitted of malpractice w/no settlement *(revenge)*

5. HECTOR—prescribed incorrect medications, secured promotion for Larry over him, threatened to have Hector's license revoked *(revenge, desperation)*

6. ELAINE—had affair with Simone while married, caused Salvador's death with malpractice and incorrect prescription, involved in medication scam, paid her cash hush money, would cut her out of will if he died *(revenge)*

7. JO—*(??)*

8. SANTINO—*(??)*

9. SUSAN—*(??)*

10. JIMMY CLAY—being blackmailed about Simone, medication scam, malpractice death *(revenge, coverup)*

11. LARRY CLAY—part of medication scam, knew about him seducing young girls *(coverup)*

Finbar sucked air through the unlit pipe and turned to the next page of Tommie's notes.

WHO HAD ACCESS TO DIGITALIS & HOW?

GERTRUDIS—Yes, Salvador's medication

KATHERINE—Yes, Larry's pharmacy

SIMONE—Yes, Dr. Frank's medication

LARA—Yes, Salvador's medication

HECTOR—Yes, Rx-All, Winn-Dixie

ELAINE—No

JO— No

SANTINO—No

SUSAN—No

JIMMY—Yes, Larry's pharmacy

LARRY—Yes, Rx-All

DR. FRANK—Yes, any pharmacy or medical facility

On the back of the page was a list of questions. Finbar read them carefully.

1. How did the victims ingest the herbs?
2. How was the Digitalis administered?
3. Why were Larry Clay and Dr. Frank holding beer if neither of them drank any?
4. Did Jimmy have a chin dimple or just Larry?
5. Were any of the victims or suspects found to have Digitalis on their skin or clothing?
6. What are we missing???

He clucked his tongue and removed his pipe and glasses after he read the last question. *What indeed, missus? What indeed?*

Chapter Twenty-Nine

TOMMIE was pleased with the outcome of her Mother's Day Tea. The sandwiches had been a big hit with both the mothers and the children. The only blot on the occasion was that Dearci, Lara, and Gertrudis had not been in attendance.

May 12 had also been Tommie's 65th birthday. Despite insisting she didn't want to celebrate, she was treated to a mini party when she returned home late that afternoon.

Finbar had strung up some colored balloons in her dining room, and Earl had provided a sumptuous strawberry covered cheesecake. The three of them feasted on dessert—cake and coffee for the men, cake and tea for her. The musical rendition of the birthday song left much

to be desired, owing to the lack of singing talent from her male companions. The dogs, however, were in great voice as they howled along.

Afterward, Finbar retired to his unit, and Tommie had been able to savor a well-deserved hour of Earl's undivided time and attention. When he finally left to finish out his shift, she had cleaned up the kitchen and climbed into bed to binge-watch the latest season of *Outlander*, which Earl had thoughtfully gifted her.

Upon arising, showering, and getting ready for her usual Monday morning, she breakfasted with Finbar.

"Thank you for yesterday. I didn't realize how much I really needed cheesecake. You're the best, Finbar. You and Earl, that is."

"Yer welcome, lad. And ye needn't always include me in yer doings, ye know. I've a mind to find m'self a woman one of these days."

"You're thinking of getting married again?"

"Jayze, woman. I thought ye knew me better. Never again will I marry, but I'm not against a little female companionship now and again, as long as the ladies goes back to their own homes."

Tommie guffawed. "Finbar, you won't do. Whatever makes you happy, though. What's on our agenda for today?"

Finbar hemmed and hawed, avoiding her eyes. "I dunno. I've got a few errands to run before coming to m'shop. What're ye thinking of doing?"

"Finbar Holmes. Have you already found a woman? Who is she?"

"No, no, lad. I have not. But we've a new neighbor moved in next door, and I thought I might take a welcome basket over. Like ye did when I moved in."

"Somebody bought that little green house next door. The one on the double lot with the huge back yard? Really? I saw they had fenced in the property."

"Aye. 'Tis but a widow lady all alone. Sherlock alerted me from the garden. He smelled her moving about from beneath the fence."

"What's she like?"

"I dunno. But I'm about finding out. Sure, sure, she may be a dried-up prune of a bitty. If she is, I'll leave the basket and be on m'way."

"And if she isn't?"

"I'll invite m'self in for a suppa tea. Regardless, I'll see ye about half ten at yer shop."

Tommie snickered at his interest in the woman next door. In one way, she was glad for him. But in another way, she felt a pang of jealousy. Since he had moved to Floribunda the past February, it had been just the two of them as fast and close friends. She hoped another woman wouldn't endanger their investigations. *Shame on you, Tommie Watson. You have a sweetheart. Why shouldn't Finbar?*

Tommie gave him a sincere smile. "I think that's a great idea, Finbar. Maybe I'll go visit the Padillas. I missed

them at the tea yesterday. You have fun. I'll be waiting to hear all about it."

"Right, then. Leave the dishes in the sink to soak, lad. 'Twill be but a wee bit, then I'll be along."

He busied himself with removing a fresh loaf of brown soda bread from the oven, and Tommie walked on out to her car. She pulled out of the driveway and headed for Greenleaf.

Fifteen minutes later, Tommie pulled up to the curb of Gertrudis Padilla's house. She looked over at Lara's mobile home and saw the car was not there. Before she even got to Gertrudis's top step, Dearci flung the door open, rushed out, and grabbed her around the waist in a bear hug.

"Miss Tommie! Miss Tommie! I've missed you."

"Hello, Dearci. I'm happy to see you, too."

"My *abuela's* in the garden. I'll go get her. Come inside. I'll be right back." The little girl ran through the door calling her grandmother's name.

Tommie stepped into the living room and looked around. She saw Dearci had been working with her herb gathering kit. Brown paper lunch sacks, blunt scissors, gloves, and an assortment of leaves, flowers, and berries were strewn over the dining room table. The child had been making sketches of her finds in a spiral bound art tablet. To Tommie's eye, they were surprisingly good for an eight-year-old.

In a few moments, Dearci ran back into the room, followed by Gertrudis Padilla carrying a wicker basket

laden with flora from her garden. She removed her wide-brimmed hat when she saw Tommie.

"Tommie Watson. What a surprise to see you. My granddaughter and I have been harvesting herbs from the garden to replenish those I used for the celebration. Please, sit down. Dearci, will you fix Ms. Watson some tea and lemon cookies while I shower off?"

Tommie shifted uncomfortably. "My visit was unexpected. I hope you don't mind me not calling."

The woman gave her a radiant smile and pushed an errant lock of hair behind her ears with a gloved hand. "You are always welcome here, Tommie. Enjoy your tea. I won't be long."

"Take your time, Gertrudis. I'll chat with Dearci while we drink our tea."

Gertrudis set her basket down on the floor and disappeared into the bathroom. Dearcilla entered the dining room with the tea tray on which sat two of the large hand decorated mugs from Jo's shop and two of the small salsa bowls with pastel yellow lemon cookies on them.

"Let's sit at the table, sweetie. You can show me what you've gathered today and your drawings."

Dearci grinned, set the tray on the table, and cleared off a spot for her guest.

"I made you a special tea with lots of agave syrup. You had agave last time you came to see us, so I know you like it. I'm having ginger ale in my mug. *Abuela* makes it from real ginger and honey and bubbly water. It's really

good. The cookies came from Walmart, but they're good, too."

Tommie inhaled the steam rising from the top of her mug. "Smells delicious. What's in it?"

"Guess!"

"OK. I smell peppermint and lavender."

"Yes, yes. What else?"

"Something citrus. Orange?"

Dearci clapped her hands. "Orange blossoms. And chocolate mint, too."

Tommie took a big sip. "I taste it. Yummy. Did you make this blend yourself?"

"Some of it. I used one *Abuela* had made, and I added some herbs and things that I like."

"Are there cloves in here?"

"Yes. I told you I liked them. And I put in a couple of broken cinnamon sticks and those star spices."

"Star anise?"

"That's the one. Do you like it?"

"It's very ... robust. Lots of flavor." Tommie pulled up the tea ball and examined it before dunking it a few times to infuse more of the essences of the blend. "You really packed it full."

"I did. More things mean more tastes for you to guess. Is there enough agave?"

"Oh, yes. Quite sweet. Thank you. Show me what you've gathered."

Dearci began opening her sacks and pulling out the

plant parts she had put in them. Some were already dried, and some were newly harvested. As she revealed each item, she told the name and what she perceived as its use. She proudly displayed her drawings, painstakingly detailed with colored pencils. Tommie offered a few minor corrections, but most of the sketches were accurate, although described in a childlike way.

"This one has pointy leaves and flowers like a yellow sun with an orange face. And this one has fat green leaves and white flowers that look like little bells. I found this one today, but I don't know what it's called." Dearci showed the sketchpad to Tommie.

"That's *Achillea millefolium*. We call it yarrow. Y-a-r-r-o-w. The yellow part in the center of the flower cluster is dried and made into a powder to put on cuts and bruises or in a tea for an upset tummy."

Tommie sipped her tea while the child wrote in her tablet. She rubbed her eyes and looked away from the drawing, unable to focus. She began to feel sluggish. *Hurry up, Gertrudis. This tea is making me sleepy, and I need to speak with you.*

As if hearing Tommie's thoughts, Gertrudis appeared and took a seat at the table.

"*Abuela*, do you want tea?" Dearci asked.

"No, dear. I've had plenty for today. What did you make for Ms. Watson?"

"I used the one with peppermint and orange. I put lots of agave. I put in some pretty flowers and spices to

make it zingy. Did I do good?"

Gertrudis patted Dearcilla on the cheek and nodded, then she turned toward Tommie, and the smile froze on her face.

"Tommie? What is it?"

"I must not have slept well last night. I feel pretty lethargic. Maybe something sugary will help." She reached for the cookies awkwardly and spilled the bowl. "Oops. Clumsy me." Her hand shook as she brought the cookie to her mouth and took a bite. Her eyes were drawn to the empty salsa bowl. *Something about that leaf ... those flowers ... that drawing.*

"You look unwell, and your pupils are quite small," Gertrudis said. "Dearci, what did you put in Ms. Watson's tea?"

The child's eyes were huge. "It was your peppermint and orange tea. I only added some spices and things."

"What did you add? What spices? What ... things did you put in it?"

Tears sprang to the little girl's eyes. "Lavender, and cinnamon, and the star spice, and cloves."

"What else?"

"Some of my pretty flowers. The purply-pink ones and the white ones and the shiny green leaves."

"Show me."

Dearci pulled leaves and flowers from her sacks.

"*Madre de Dios.*" Gertrudis spoke in a whisper.

Tommie's vision clouded as she listened to Dearci and Gertrudis talking. They seemed far away. *If I could just lie down and sleep, I think I'd feel better.*

That was her last thought as her eyes closed and she slid from the chair.

Chapter Thirty

TOMMIE'S lids fluttered open, and she found herself looking directly into two steely grey eyes beneath bushy white brows. Slowly, Earl's face came into focus.

"Darlin'? Tommie? I thought I'd lost you for good," he said. Putting the thought into words made his eyes begin to water. He blinked away the tears and snuffed.

"What happened? Where am I?" she asked. Her voice was barely a whisper.

"You're at the Urgent Care Clinic."

"I ... I was so sleepy ... and I ... just went away."

"You were poisoned, Tommie."

"What? Who?" She struggled to remember where she had been. "Gertrudis poisoned me?"

"No. Gertrudis actually saved your life. If she

hadn't forced that herbal potion down your throat. You'd have died in her house."

"Who, then? Not Dearci."

"Dearcilla called 9-1-1."

"The tea. Too strong. Bitter aftertaste. The flavors all wrong."

"Yes, it was the tea."

Finbar appeared in Tommie's line of sight.

"Finbar? Were you there?"

"No, lad. Yer man called me. I should have gone with ye instead of making a silly social visit. Can ye ever forgive me, Thomasina?"

"Always forgive you. But so confused."

"Ye should be. Ye nearly left me, missus. Ye nearly left all of us."

"Pinpoint pupils. Lethargy. Slow heart rate. Blurred vision. Disorientation. Drowsiness. Stomachache."

"What's that, missus?"

"Speckled purplish flowers. White bell-shaped flowers. Broad, glossy green leaves."

"Darlin'?" Earl said. "What are you telling me?"

"She's out of her head again, lad," Finbar said.

Tommie clenched Earl's hand. "No garlic smell."

"Garlic? In the tea?" he asked.

She closed her eyes and wiped her other hand on her throat. "Not Ransoms garlic. Thirsty. I taste charcoal."

Finbar grabbed the cup with the bendy straw and put it to her lips. "The doctor said drink plenty of water."

Tommie took several swallows and drained the cup. Finbar replenished the water, and she took a few more sips before pulling away.

"Careless of me. There all the time. Right in front of me. Toxic plants. The mugs. The bowls."

"Missus, are ye telling me the ceramics had toxic plants in them?"

"*On* them. Dearci's decorations. Put them in the tea. I drank them."

"The lassie tried to poison ye?" Finbar was aghast.

"No. Just a child. Didn't know they were toxic."

Earl smoothed her hair and kissed her forehead. "I know, darlin'. I've talked with Gertrudis Padilla. She recognized your symptoms and gave you a potion, some activated charcoal, and her homemade ginger ale. When she examined her granddaughter's herb kit, she found foxglove flowers and lily of the valley flowers. The salsa dishes each had a full lily of the valley leaf inlaid into the bowl."

"Dearci didn't mean to," Tommie croaked.

"No, she didn't. It wasn't her fault. Her grandmother should have been more conscious of what the girl was collecting."

"Not her fault, either. Kids do what kids do."

"And I do what I do. Gertrudis will be charged with negligence and use of a harmful substance." A muscle throbbed in his temple.

"No, Earl. Don't go off half-cocked. I'm OK. I'll be fine."

"You almost died, damnit. She can't be allowed to practice herbal medicine if she can't even supervise her own grandchild. It's dangerous and unethical."

"Dangerous. Unethical. Like Dr. Frank and Larry Clay? Their behavior was intentional. Gertrudis's was not."

"What would you have me do, Tommie?"

"Breathe. Wait."

"Wait for what? Someone else to die?"

"No. Let me think. No tea at the *Cinco de Mayo* thing. Salsa bowls. The glaze gave them protection. Except ... except a broken bowl would expose the leaf. Jimmy Clay broke the bowl. Drank the salsa. Ate the leaf."

"Yer right, lad. He ate the poisonous plant. But the others? They didn't," Finbar said.

"Dearci. Must've decorated their salsa. She added flowers before Lara stopped her. An accidental poisoning."

"That makes perfect sense, but it's still her grandmother's carelessness for allowing her access to those plants," Earl said.

"Gertrudis rid her garden of both foxglove and lily of the valley. Burned them in the woods. Dearci went to the woods. They must have regrown out there," Tommie said.

Earl breathed a deep sigh. "Still ..."

"Yes. I agree. Gertrudis must have better supervision. What if Dearci had consumed them?"

"Exactly. So, what should I do about it?"

"Warn her, but don't arrest her. Please?"

"Damnit, Tommie!"

"Dangit, Earl."

"What am I going to do with you? You are the most infuriating, headstrong ..."

"... loveable, charming ..."

"...wonderful thing to come into my life."

"I know. Love you, too. Now let me rest. Have to solve three murders, you know."

Earl dropped his jaw, then he fixed his eyes on Finbar and scowled.

"Don't look at me, lad. She's *yer* woman," he said.

Chapter Thirty-One

EARL sat in Sanderson's office that afternoon nursing a hot cup of coffee. He had just told his coroner friend the details of Tommie's brush with death and the toxic herbs she ingested at the Padilla house.

"My gosh, Earl. That could've been the end for her." Sandy drained his cup and wiped his mouth with his hand. "I need a refill. How about you?"

"I'm good. You go ahead."

Sandy ambled out the door and returned with a hot, steaming cup. "I'd say that gives us an explanation for the plant toxins. And the mother confirmed the child added hawthorn berry and Siberian ginseng, as well. Combined with the interactions from the bananas and black licorice, it accounts for the natural digoxin in all three bodies."

"Yup. It doesn't account for the *Digitalis*, though."

"I've reviewed the files, looking for any clues to that, and I think I may have something. I wanted to be sure before I released the bodies to the families for internment."

"Is there something from their autopsies?"

"Their toxicologies are consistent with the plants and the pharmaceuticals. And, of course, Jimmy Clay was drunk on his feet, but the other two revealed no alcohol."

"Tommie said there were multiple bottles of beer at the table, and Larry had one in his hand."

"That may well be, but the only one who drank them was Jimmy Clay. I wish we had collected the bottles to check for trace, but I'm sorry to say we neglected to because of the preponderance of beer bottles in the vicinity of the table." Sandy shook his head. "That's on me."

"It happens, Sandy. We miss things."

"Yeah, I know. I neglected to tell you all three men had recently been treated for intimate contact disease."

"That's pretty disgusting."

"I agree, but I've seen it in people from all walks of life. Dr. Le did find some interesting things on the clothing and on the hands of the victims that he noted in his report."

"Such as?"

"Such as ... let me find it ... Ah, here. Fingernail scrapings from Dr. Frank revealed *Digitalis* powder. That didn't catch my attention at first because I knew Dr. Frank had an underlying condition that he treated with *Digitalis*. It was entirely normal for him to have it both in his system

and on his hands."

"What makes it suspicious now?"

"There was evidence of it in his left side trouser pocket. When one takes that kind of medication, it is in a specific regimen, that is, the same time every day. There's no reason to bring it along in your pocket. It's not like nitroglycerine tabs that you would take if you were going into heart failure. Doesn't work that way. So why have it in your slacks that have just come from the cleaners?"

"How do you know his pants had just come from the cleaners?

"There was a tag stapled inside the waistband from Fluff and Fold Laundry and Dry Cleaners."

"Maybe he had a pill in there before he took his pants to Fluff and Fold."

"Then the pill would have dissolved and left a sticky residue in the pocket. Dr. Le also found a small scrap of paper napkin."

"From the celebration?"

"No. Different material. They used coarse brown paper towels in Greenleaf that Sunday. This was soft and white. I believe the pill … or pills … had been wrapped in the napkin prior to being placed in his pocket."

"Why?"

Sandy locked eyes with Earl. "That's a particularly good question, my friend. Furthermore, the *Digitalis* was in loose powder form … what you'd normally find inside gelatin capsules."

"Wow. He intended to add it to something and wanted it to act quicker than letting the capsules dissolve."

"That's exactly what I'm thinking. But what?"

"Someone's food? Maybe a beer? Hmm?"

"Bingo! You win."

"So, you think Dr. Frank was going to use it to poison somebody. Who?"

"I don't know. But listen to this." Sandy picked up another folder and opened it. "Larry Clay also had *Digitalis* beneath his fingernails and in his shirt pocket."

"What? Was it a powder, too?"

"No. It was a tablet, and it had been broken. Dr. Le found a tiny piece of it still in the pocket."

"Did he have a heart condition?"

"No, he did not. So, why did he have a *Digitalis* tablet in his pocket?"

"Damned if I know. Don't tell me Jimmy Clay had in on his hands or in his clothes, too."

"No. Only in his system. Now, get this. The *Digitalis* in Dr. Frank's pocket we've identified as *Cardiotalis*. It was from a 0.25mg capsule manufactured by a company out of India. I believe there may have been more than one capsule, judging from the amount of powder found in the creases of the pocket. That was his prescribed medication. The *Digitalis* tablet in Larry Clay's pocket was identified as *Digicardio*, a 0.25mg tablet manufactured in the USA. It was not a medication prescribed for him."

"What in the holy hell is going on?"

"I don't know, Earl. But here's the kicker. The *Digitalis* found in Jimmy Clay's system was *Cardiotalis and Digicardio and* a generic form of digoxin.

Earl sat still and chewed the inside of his mouth before speaking again. "Sandy. Did Dr. Frank *and* Larry Clay poison Jimmy Clay? Is that what you're telling me?"

"I think they did, Earl. I think they did."

"But what about the generic form of digoxin?"

"Earl, I have absolutely no idea where that came from, but none was found on Dr. Frank or Larry Clay. It *was,* however, in Dr. Frank's system."

"So, a third person contributed to Jimmy Clay's death in addition to Dr. Frank?"

"It would appear so, buddy. It would appear so."

Chapter Thirty-Two

TOMMIE was released from the Urgent Care Clinic on Tuesday. Finbar took her home and made frequent trips back and forth between their units to be sure she was well hydrated and lacked for nothing.

He left a note on his shop door that Caife Caife Holmes would be closed for the remainder of the week but would serve dinner on the weekend. He posted the menu and asked those who wished to make reservations to leave a message on his voicemail. At Tommie's request, he also posted a CLOSED notice on her shop.

That evening, he and Tommie gathered in her living room to compare their case files. Earl had called and apprised Finbar of Sandy's toxicology findings in and on the bodies. Now, it was up to Holmes and Watson,

Investigators to put their puzzle-solving heads together and make sense of the clues. Finbar had even brought over his empty pipe. With the three dogs lounging contentedly on the floor, Tommie and Finbar began to work their magic to solve the crimes.

"… and Lara told her mother that Dearci added the pretty flowers—not knowing they were toxic— to the salsa for Larry Clay because he was kind to her at the booth. She said he patted her head and complimented her on her pretty eyes and cute dimples. He even pointed at his face to show her he had an identical chin dimple! That's when Gertrudis knew he was Dearci's father instead of Jimmy. Jimmy had no chin dimple," Tommie said.

"And Dr. Frank was kind to her, as well, so he received decorative flowers in his salsa."

"Right. The women were cranky and dismissive, so she didn't adorn their salsa."

"So that explains why Jo Clay was given a bowl with flowers. The lass likes her quite well."

"Yes. She put a lot more flowers on Jo's salsa. Then Jimmy broke the bowl, slurped up the contents, and ate the leaf protruding from the jagged edge."

"Brute. Served him right, in my opinion."

"And that exonerates Jo as far as means and motive." Tommie shifted her position on the chaise.

"Do ye need something, missus?"

"No, just getting more comfortable. Where was I? Oh, yeah. According to Sandy, both Dr. Frank and Larry

Clay had brought prescription *Digitalis* with them to the *Cinco de Mayo* celebration."

"Correct. Are we of the belief they each intended to poison Jimmy Clay?"

"Yep. He had both brands of *Digitalis* in his system, which had to have been added to something he ate or drank. My thinking is, because of the beers on the table, they each dosed a bottle."

"It would appear that way. D'you think they were in collusion? Or d'you think they added it independently of one another?"

"See, that's the funny thing. They both had motive to get rid of him."

"True. Their women had been bedded by the lout and had been transmitted a condition they then passed on to their respective housemates. Could there be a stronger motive, d'you think?"

"Jimmy Clay was known for digging up dirt and blackmailing people. Maybe he was blackmailing them, as well as Simone and Katherine."

"Missus. Ye told me Elaine said Larry Clay was part of the scheme with Dr. Frank to overmedicate patients, which ultimately resulted in Mr. Padilla's death. Perhaps the brother knew it and was blackmailing them about it."

"That's a good theory. Unfortunately, we don't have any proof. But I'm willing to bet he was."

"Shall we discuss the findings yer cousin related to you concerning the disparity of the poisons the men

ingested and the poisons they had on them?"

"Let's. Jimmy Clay was dosed with Cardiotalis, Digicardio, and generic digoxin. Larry Clay ingested Cardiotalis only. Dr. Frank had Cardiotalis and generic digoxin in his system."

"Cardiotalis is what the chemist prescribed for Dr. Frank. It would have been already in his blood. By my deduction, Dr. Frank administered his prescription to Larry Clay and Jimmy Clay."

"That deduction would fit. Larry Clay had Digicardio on him but not in his system. He had to have given it to Dr. Frank and Jimmy Clay."

"And both Jimmy Clay and Dr. Frank had generic digoxin in their system. But none of the men possessed it."

"So, since Larry Clay had only Cardiotalis in his system, it stands to reason that Dr. Frank killed him."

"Precisely."

"But I can't figure out why. And I don't know why Larry Clay would've given the Digicardio to Dr. Frank."

"Perhaps to silence the partner in crime. Perhaps by accident. We have no way of knowing because the men can never tell us."

Tommie grumbled. "Dangitall. I hate loose ends."

"As you say, lad. Because Jimmy Clay had both prescription medications in his system, I deduce that Dr. Frank and his brother Larry Clay poisoned him."

"I agree, and I completely understand why *he* was killed. He was the worst human being ever."

"The rub comes with the third poison, Thomasina. The generic digoxin."

"Right. Who dispensed that?"

"I checked with Tom Beadwell, and he stated the Rx-All does not carry generic medications."

"What? I thought all pharmacies have generic options. Isn't one reason Hector lost the promotion because he gave people more affordable medications? Didn't he tell us he dispensed generic substitutions?"

"Not exactly. He said he offered over-the-counter options and wholistic alternatives."

"Then, if the Rx-All doesn't carry generic brands, it must have come from another pharmacy."

Tommie and Finbar locked eyes.

"Winn-Dixie," they said simultaneously.

Chapter Thirty-Three

FINBAR answered a knock at Tommie's door and was delighted to see their friends Elaine, Susan, Don, and Henry bearing takeout sacks.

"Halloo, friends. We're happy to have yer company. I see ye brought some refreshments. Lovely. Come, set them out, and I'll collect our plates."

The Fab Four placed the sacks on the table. Elaine and Susan immediately ran to Tommie and hugged her while the men busied themselves in her kitchen arranging the food on the table, along with a pitcher of iced Red Rooibos tea from Tommie's refrigerator.

"We were told you liked the *Solar System Sub Sandwich Sampler.* We do, too," Don said.

"Sid and Jeanette comped it. We're The Lunch

Pad's new delivery assistants," Henry said with a laugh.

"But ye will stay and eat with us," Finbar said.

"Absolutely!"

"Sisters, Tommie. Do you want to eat in the dining room or in the living room?" Don asked.

Susan answered him. "We'll fix our plates and eat here. Y'all take the table. Come on, Tommie,"

Elaine helped Tommie up to the fixings and carried her plate back to the chaise, along with a glass of cold tea. She served herself, and then she took a place on the loveseat while Susan perched on the leather chair across from them. The men settled themselves at the table.

"What's in the sack ye put in the ice box, Henry?" Finbar asked.

"Oh, that's something special we picked up at the store. We heard Tommie had a birthday, and we got a cake for dessert."

Don grinned. "A little birdie told us you liked cheesecake. We wanted it to stay cool until after lunch."

"Y'all are so thoughtful." Tommie clapped her hands. "Cheesecake is my absolute favorite."

"So the big birdie told us." Susan giggled.

"Is the birdie tall with a white beard and grey eyes?" Tommie asked.

"For cripes sake, Tommie. Who else would it be?" Elaine said.

The women collapsed into a paroxysm of laughter as the men rolled their eyes.

Tommie regained her composure. "Elaine. I never got around to finding out about Dr. Frank's will."

"Oh, that was a shock, let me tell you. He left his entire estate to me because I was 'the faithful wife.' What do you think of that?"

"What about Simone?"

"Left her out completely. She was livid. I thought she was going to explode. She said some French words … I'm assuming they were curse words … and shouted at Harvey Lassiter. I'm surprised he didn't fire her on the spot. But, you know, she was grieving and all that, so he cut her some slack, I guess."

Susan wiped the corner of her mouth. "Not to mention, sister, now that Norman's out of the picture, Harvey may figure Simone will sleep with him again."

Elaine's eyes snapped wide open. "Sister! That's an ugly thing to say. Ugly … but true, bless her heart."

Tommie snickered at the euphemism. "Finbar said Katherine was at the law office, too. Did she come to your ex-husband's will reading?"

"No, she was in another room. But I take it she was none too pleased with the outcome of her husband's will and insurance. His beneficiary was Dearcilla Padilla."

"Finbar told me. Guess we know why."

Susan's face paled. "It makes me sick to my stomach. Not for the child, but because Larry was so depraved, he had sex with a teenager. I suspected, though. He paid way too much attention to her. You never want to

believe things like that of your husband, but once you see it and you know in your heart it's true, you can never, ever be with that person again. It still makes me feel so foolish."

"Susan, you're not the first woman to be deceived and still stand by her man. I did that, too, with one of my husbands. I spent years being embarrassed that he fathered another woman's child while married to me. Spent lots of money on counseling, too. Eventually, I had to say, 'that's on him' and get over it," Tommie said.

"Thanks, Tommie. That makes me feel better."

"Good. And, if you want, Susan, I can give you my therapist's number. He's top notch. By the way, Elaine, do you know if Larry left Katherine any kind of financial compensation? I understand they were divorcing but it wasn't final."

"Oh, they were divorcing, all right. She was asking for everything, and he was giving her nothing."

"No alimony, even?"

"Why should he? She has a job at Kitty Kare. I don't know what a bookkeeper makes there, but she supported herself before she married him, so she could support herself afterward, too."

"Sister, that's harsh," Susan said.

"For cripes sake, Tommie, give her your therapist's number! Sister, Larry gave you pittance, and then he even quit giving you that. Don't you dare feel sorry for Katherine or Larry, either one!"

"Who wants cake?" Finbar asked, getting to his

feet quickly and approaching the refrigerator.

The sisters awkwardly raised their hands, silently apologizing to each other with their eyes. Tommie shot her arm up, as well.

Finbar brought the plastic sack out and set it on the counter. When he pushed the sides down, he exposed a large pre-sliced cheesecake. Three of the slices were topped with shaved chocolate, three were covered with cherries in a shiny glaze, three were drizzled with caramel, and three were plain. He described them to the guests and took orders, serving them on small saucers. He set the remaining cake back in the refrigerator. When he went back to the counter, he found another bag inside the sack.

"Halloo! What's this?" he asked.

"Oh, that's mine," Henry said. "It's some medication for my cat."

"Ye have a feline, Henry? I did not know that."

Henry grinned. "Yeah, the sisters gave him to me after ... well, after Coral and Beverly died. They said he would be good company. And they were right. Rufus is a good ole cat."

"Where'd you get him, sisters? Is there a pet store in town?" Tommie asked.

"Oh, no. He's a rescue from the shelter. We don't support dog and cat mills. That's where most pet stores get their animals," Susan said.

"The shelter ... meaning Kitty Kare?"

"Yes. They take excellent care of their cats."

"Henry, ye said it was medicine. What's wrong with the wee lad?" Finbar asked.

"He has to take something to keep his heart rhythm stable. It beats too fast sometimes."

Finbar opened the bag and looked inside. "May I?"

Henry nodded, and Finbar removed the small white plastic bottle. A plastic syringe with a squeeze bulb was taped to the side. He read the label aloud.

"Rufus. One ml twice daily." He looked at Tommie. "Digoxin."

"Where did ya'll get the cheesecake … and the cat's medicine?" Tommie asked.

The four guests all answered at the same time. "Winn Dixie."

Chapter Thirty-Four

TOMMIE AND FINBAR spent an uneventful Wednesday at home. They munched on leftover sandwich fixings and cheesecake and continued to fill out their case files.

Earl called Tommie in the afternoon and told her Hector Flores had been arrested in connection with the murder of Jimmy Clay and Dr. Norman Frank. Though it signaled a successful close to the investigation, Tommie felt disquieted. Finbar was not at home, so she could not discuss her feelings with him. He was next door with the new neighbor woman Tommie had yet to meet. Sherlock had taken up residence on the loveseat, along with Zed and Red.

Tommie served herself another slice of cheesecake and sat poring over her notes. By all intents and purposes, Hector Flores was the ideal suspect. He had strong motive

to kill all three men, he had means, and he had opportunity. Hector had no alibi for the crimes. He was present at the celebration, he had contact with the victims, and he had direct access to both brands of prescription *Digitalis* and generic digoxin.

As far as motives were concerned, Jimmy Clay spread diseases all around town, and Larry gave him free medication, passing off the discrepancies in the books as Hector's fault. Larry Clay cost him his promotion, and the only way he could advance and recover his position was for Larry to be out of the way. Dr. Frank and Larry devised the scheme to overcharge customers by prescribing and dispensing large quantities of expensive medication which were billed at regular cost, but which went directly into the two men's pockets—the shortages being attributed to Hector's mismanagement. Dr. Frank convinced Tom Beadwell to promote Larry and cut Hector's hours. To add insult to injury, he threatened to have Hector's license revoked for dispensing alternative medicines.

Sanderson Harper confirmed the generic digoxin was likely administered in liquid form. Its presence in Dr. Frank's stomach contents was confined to the *Tamales Carnitas Flores* ... the pork tamales served by Hector and Carmine Flores. When confronted with that fact, Earl told Tommie that Hector broke down into tears while still proclaiming his innocence.

The dogs awoke when the doorbell rang. Tommie quieted them and looked through the peephole. She was

startled to see Katherine Clay and Simone Lorence outside on the porch. Remembering the episode when Louanne Weller posed as a food delivery person and attacked her when she opened her door, Tommie left the chain on and spoke through the crack.

"Simone. Katherine. What are you doing here?"

"Oh, Tommie. We are zo zorry to hear of your unfortunate accident. Ze child could have killed you wide zat poizon," Simone trilled.

"It was exactly that, Simone ... an accident."

"*Mais oui.* But ze world would not be Ze zame widzout Tommie Watzon."

"We brought you a card, Tommie, and some homemade lemonade. It's made with organic lemons and tupelo honey." Katherine thrust the card and the gallon jug toward the door.

"Thank you, Katherine. I do like lemonade ... especially with honey." Tommie opened the crack enough to grab the quart-sized glass jug. "I'd invite y'all in, but I'm ... um ... still in my pajamas. I appreciate y'all stopping by." She smiled and pushed the door closed, watching through the peephole as the two women sauntered away.

Tommie set the jug on the table, opened the envelope, and withdrew a run-of-the-mill get-well card signed by Simone and Katherine. *Wow. A lot of thought went into this sentiment, ladies.* She rolled her eyes and returned to her notes.

The dogs suddenly retreated out the portal with a

blam-blam-blam. Tommie smiled. *Finbar's home.* For some unknown reason, an old song flashed through her mind. *Froggie went a-courtin' and he did ride, uh huh.*

When Finbar entered her kitchen door, she was still laughing.

"What's got ye so giddy, missus?"

"Nothing. Funny song I remembered. Did you have a nice visit next door?"

"I did. Lovely woman. Her name is Marilee. Marilee Nesmyth. Spelled with a Y; pronounced as an I. She grows and sells organic vegetables without commercial pesticides. Markets her own natural product and calls it 'Godiva's Garden-Grow.' Isn't that grand?"

"Yeah. That's great, Finbar. Nesmyth, huh? That's an unusual name."

"Her husband was British. She's moved here from London. Ye would like her, Thomasina."

"I'm sure I will. Right now, though, I'm puzzling out this investigation."

"Are ye, now? Did we not agree that Hector Flores committed the crimes?"

"We did, but I feel like we missed something crucial. After talking with him, do you really feel, deep down, that he could do such a thing?"

"I dunno. The facts surely point to it, but yer right. In m'heart of hearts, I fail to see him as a calculating murderer." He took a glass from her cabinet and walked toward the table. "Did ye make a lemon smash, missus?"

"A what? Lemon smash? OK, I suppose that makes sense. Here we call it lemonade."

"Righto. Fancy a glass?" He poured himself one.

"No, not right now. I didn't make it, by the way. Katherine Clay and Simone Lorence brought it by."

"Jayze. Who would've thought that? Have ye been friendly with them in the past, lad?"

"No. Never. It's odd they gave me a get-well card and a gift. They don't like me ... or you, for that matter."

Finbar shrugged and brought the glass to his lips.

"STOP!" Tommie shouted. "Don't drink it!"

Finbar nearly dropped the glass. "What're ye on about, Thomasina. I've smash all over m'self now." He grabbed a kitchen towel and blotted his face and shirt.

"I may be crazy, but I don't trust them. I'd rather let Sandy take a sample first. If I'm right, I may have solved these murders. Give me a minute to grab my flip-flops, then take me to the coroner's office. Close that jug and bring it."

"As ye say, Thomasina. If yer hunch is right, I owe ye m'life, lad."

"Turnabout's fair play, my friend. Let's go."

Chapter Thirty-Five

EARL'S FACE progressed from tan to white to red after Sandy reentered the office and presented his findings. The examination of the contents of the jug revealed water, lemons, honey, ... and digoxin.

Earl clasped Tommie's hand tightly. "You were right, darlin'. You were right."

"There's enough digoxin in this lemonade to cause sudden cardiac arrest in two people. Assuming you and Finbar each had two glasses, you'd likely have died before you realized what was happening. You'd have felt dizzy at first, and the second glass would've compounded the effects of the digoxin enough to cause a heart attack." Sandy said.

"Jayze." Finbar ran his hands through his thin hair.

Earl leaned over, gathered Tommie in a bear hug,

and pulled her cheek to his lips. When he leaned back, there was a fierceness in his eyes she had never seen.

"I'm OK, Earl. I'm OK."

"Yup. And you're gonna stay that way. Finbar, take Tommie home, and the two of you stay there. Don't let anybody inside. Sandy, let's us go on over to the station so I can get arrest warrants out for Katherine Clay and Simone Lorence."

"And Hector Flores?" Tommie questioned.

"I'm cutting him loose."

*   *   *

Earl arrived at Tommie's house that evening with a bouquet of flowers. He had called ahead to tell her he was bringing dinner from *Mucho Mexicale,* so Finbar didn't have to prepare anything. The three of them avoided conversation about the case until they had finished their meal and retired to the living room with drinks. Finbar and Earl drank from cold cans of Guinness beer, and Tommie sipped a glass of her iced herbal tea.

"Can you talk about it now, Earl?" Tommie asked.

He laid his large hand on her thigh and nodded.

"For the most part, your investigation uncovered the essential facts. Simone and Katherine were the missing details. We arrested them, and they confessed. Well, let me clarify. Katherine confessed and rolled on Simone."

"Really? What did she say?"

"Simone was the instigator. She had a fling with Jimmy Clay, and he gave her a disease that she passed on to Norman Frank. Norman had not been with another woman, so when he found out he had a condition of a personal nature, he knew he got it from Simone. He was furious, and he told her he was going to change his will to leave everything to Elaine Frank who had never been unfaithful to him."

"Ironic, isn't it. He cheated on Elaine. Simone cheated on him. Then, he leaves his estate to the ex-wife."

"Strange, but true. The weird thing was that Jimmy was blackmailing Simone and saying he would tell Dr. Frank. She didn't tell the doctor Jimmy Clay was the man she had been with, but Jimmy himself did."

"That must have undone him," Finbar remarked.

"More than that," Earl said. "It made him hopping mad, not only with Simone and Jimmy, but with Larry."

"Why Larry?" Tommie asked.

"Because Larry knew how Jimmy was. He called him a 'serial sexer.' Norman knew Larry gave Jimmy meds on a regular basis because he kept getting infected."

"Ew. So nasty."

"Yup. At the same time, Jimmy had an affair with Katherine Clay and ..."

"... gave her the same disease, which she gave to her husband," Finbar said.

"Right. Oddly enough, Larry had been faithful to Katherine, especially after he realized he was Dearcilla

Padilla's natural father. He cleaned up his act—and his face, apparently—in an attempt to have the little girl in his life. Katherine said he had offered Lara money to allow him to share custody of Dearci. Katherine, on the other hand, went behind his back and *did* give money to Lara to *not* give him custody."

"This is so convoluted."

"Wait, darlin'. You ain't heard convoluted yet. There's much more to this sordid little story. Your minor characters had a variety of motives. Jo Clay, Santino Alvarez, Gertrudis and Lara Padilla, Hector Flores, and even Elaine Frank. But the major players were Simone Lorence, Katherine Clay, Larry Clay, and Norman Frank. And the intended victim was Jimmy Clay. They all wanted him dead."

"Then how did yer man Larry Clay and yer man Norman Frank end up dead?" Finbar asked.

"Here's what happened. The night of the *Cinco de Mayo* celebration came along, and both couples attended. Simone and Norman were fighting. Larry and Katherine were fighting. And Jimmy Clay was running loose wreaking havoc in Greenfield.

"Larry Clay stole *Digicardio* tablets from the Rx-All pharmacy with the intention of killing his brother. They were broken into small pieces and kept inside his shirt pocket. He added the drug to Jimmy's beer, or I should say beers. Jimmy drank three bottles of beer, each laced with a broken tablet of *Digicardio*.

"Norman Frank had a heart condition and was taking *Cardiotalis*. He opened several of his capsules and poured the powder into a paper napkin, which he kept in his pants pocket. He added part of the powder into one of the beer bottles and the rest into a bowl of *pico de gallo* salsa, which he set at Jimmy's seat. Jimmy drank the beer, but Larry ate Jimmy's salsa."

"You've gotta be kidding me," Tommie said.

Earl crossed his heart. "I promise you, I'm not. In the meantime, Katherine Clay had stolen twelve bottles of digoxin from the refrigerator at the Kitty Kare."

"Did they not notice a dozen missing bottles?" Finbar asked.

"No. She had been gathering them a couple a day for a week."

"For what purpose, lad?"

"To kill Jimmy Clay ... and to give to Simone."

"For Simone?" Tommie said.

"Yup. Simone planned to kill Dr. Frank before he changed his will. And she had talked Katherine into agreeing that they had to get rid of Jimmy Clay."

"Katherine went along with it?"

"She did, darlin'. She did. So, now, the rest of the story. Simone and Katherine each had four bottles of digoxin, and they were methodical in how they used them.

"Simone bought a beer from the vendor and poured two bottles of digoxin into it before she got to the table. She didn't know Larry was also going to dose the

beer, but that's kindof a moot point, I guess. She poured the other two bottles into Dr. Frank's soft drink can.

"Katherine poured two bottles onto the chicken empanadas Jimmy had been eating and poured her last two bottles onto the pork tamales she bought from Hector and Carmine Flores. She put the plate at Jimmy's seat. Unfortunately, when Jimmy walked away from it to assault Jo, Dr. Frank ate it instead."

"Talk about overkill!" Tommie said. "Did Katherine intend to kill Larry?"

"No. She had resigned herself to the divorce because she figured she would get half of the marital assets. After he died, she thought she'd be his insurance beneficiary. She was devastated when she learned he left his money to Dearci."

"Live by the sword. Die by the sword," Finbar said.

"What's that, Holmes?"

"An old adage. If ye live by the sword, ye will die by the sword. Jimmy Clay's sword was his indiscretion and assault on women. Larry Clay's sword was his appetite for a young girl and his adultery. Dr. Frank's sword was his misuse of his medical profession."

Earl nodded appreciatively. "Good points, Holmes. Jimmy's sword was also blackmailing. Simone and Katherine unwisely revealed, through pillow talk, about the overmedication scam hatched by Larry and the doctor. That, even more than him bedding their women, was the ultimate reason the men decided to kill him. They could

stand the loss of wife and girlfriend, but not the loss of their additional livelihood."

Tommie eased herself into Earl's arms and rested against his chest. "Good old-fashioned greed. Common motive. Earl, what will happen to Simone and Katherine? And what about Katherine's sons?"

"Katherine will be charged with accessory to murder and conspiracy to commit murder. The last four bottles of digoxin were in the lemonade they brought for you and Finbar. They were desperate to shut y'all up."

Everyone sat quietly for a moment digesting that piece of information before Earl continued.

"The State Attorney has decided to ask for a reduced sentence for Katherine because she cooperated and gave Simone up. She might get probation, but I think she may have to spend several years in prison first. The father of the boys will be awarded custody, since they're still minors in middle school.

"Simone will be charged with murder in the first degree, accessory to murder, and attempted murder. Her actions were premeditated. I don't doubt that she will spend 25 years to life in prison. She will never see France." Earl winked. "She's not really French, you know,"

"We know," Finbar and Tommie said together.

Chapter Thirty-Six

EARL AND TOMMIE held hands as they sat in the folding chairs set up in the open barn. Beside them sat Finbar and his new lady friend, Marilee Nesmyth, but they did not hold hands. The barn was filled to capacity with guests from both the Floribunda and Greenleaf communities.

Muller's Animal Farm had been chosen as the venue for the May 18 weddings. Friends of the couples had spent hours decorating the barn with balloons, streamers, twinkle lights, and flowers. Even the small animals were a part of the festivities as they cavorted inside their fenced-off areas wearing fresh edible flowers and greens as "corsages" and "boutonnieres."

Refreshments were set up in an adjacent pop-up tent with crudités prepared by Tommie and Finbar,

sandwiches and cold salads from The Lunch Pad brought by Sid and Jeanette Spock, and drinks in large, galvanized buckets of ice provided by Don, Henry, Elaine, and Susan. Gifts for the happy couples filled tables in another tent.

Vocals for the event were provided by Tina Brass, Joan Carroll, and Annie Lang, accompanied by prerecorded music played on a karaoke machine. Their renditions, in three-part harmony, set the mood for the ceremonies.

The guests quieted as the trio sang, and the first couple walked down the center aisle to the front to meet the officiator. Sanderson Harper, a duly authorized notary public, began the nuptials.

"We are gathered today to bear witness to the marriage of Santino Juan Alvarez to Joanne Lee Clay."

Santino and Jo beamed at each other while he continued. As soon as he said the words, "I pronounce you husband and wife," the couple kissed and moved to stand at the side.

The trio sang another song, and the second couple walked the aisle. Sandy began the introduction.

"We are gathered today to bear witness to the marriage of Leo Manuel Alvarez to Ellissa Ann James."

Leo and Elly faced each other and held hands tightly until Sandy pronounced them husband and wife. Leo grabbed her for a longer-than-suggested kiss, and the crowd applauded.

Earl and Tommie scarcely let go of each other's hands long enough to clap. As the Songbirds warbled their

last song, they returned their attention to the canopied front staging area.

Sandy smiled broadly and spoke to the crowd.

"We are gathered today to bear witness to the marriage of Levi Joseph Muller and Aubrey Goldie Rush."

At the end of the vows, Sandy laid a handkerchief -wrapped glass on the floor. Levi and Aubrey stamped on it and broke the glass.

"What God hath joined together, let no man put asunder. I present to you our newlyweds—Santino and Jo Alvarez, Leo and Elly Alvarez, and Levi and Aubrey Muller."

Watson's Herbal Teas & Potions

Herbal information offered in the Holmes & Watson Culinary Whodunit series is for entertainment purposes only. Patent Print Books and Michelle Busby make no medical claims, nor do they intend to diagnose, treat, cure, or prevent any disease or medical condition. Teas, tonics, and potions prepared in the fictional Watson's Reme-teas have not been evaluated by the Food and Drug Administration. Readers must do their own research concerning the safety and usage of any herbs or supplements which appear in the books.

NOTE: PLEASE HEED THE WARNINGS IN [BRACKETS!]
USED INCORRECTLY, HERBS CAN BE DEADLY AS POISONS!

TO MAKE TEA: Unless otherwise noted, measure equal amounts of each herb, and combine in a large bowl. Mix thoroughly. Fill one tea strainer or infuser ball with 1-2 TBS of herb mixture and put in cup or mug. Pour 6-8 ounces of boiled water over the herbs and allow to steep for 5-10 minutes. Remove herbs. Add sweeteners, cream, or lemon as desired. (TOMMIE'S TIP: Any herb may be omitted. For stronger tea, you may bruise or grind the herbs before adding. Store herbs in an airtight container away from heat and light. Tommie encourages the use of natural or organic sweeteners.)

Natural or Organic Sweeteners

100% grade A dark maple syrup
Agave - blue, red, or gold
Raw honey
Vanilla
Stevia
Molasses
Monk fruit
Coconut sugar
Raw turbinado sugar

Cinnamon/all-spice/nutmeg

Dreamer Creamer

Combine ingredients and refrigerate before use.
Nutmeg, ½ tsp, ground
Rose water, 1 TBS
[AVOID if pregnant or breastfeeding]
Fresh milk or cream, 8 oz.

Stevanilla

Scrape seeds from vanilla bean into powdered stevia to infuse flavor.
Sift out seeds before using in tea.
Vanilla beans, dried
Powdered stevia

Rumbly Tummy Reme-Tea

Bruise/crush flowers, leaves, and seeds. Add boiling water to
steep 5 minutes. Sweeten with honey.
Drink warm tea before/after meals, as needed
Peppermint leaves & flowers
Dill leaves & seeds
Raw tupelo honey

Minty May Day Matcha

Matcha powder (¼)
Spearmint leaves (2)
Peppermint leaves (2)
Grated Cinnamon (¼)

Lemon-Lime Llama Tea

Lemongrass
Lemon balm
Lemon verbena
Mexican lime (key lime) leaves
Grated Lime peel
Grated Lemon peel

Té de Flores Rosado (Rosy Flowers Tea)

Red Rooibos tea
Hibiscus flowers
Red Rose Petals (½)
[AVOID if pregnant or breastfeeding; omit if headache occurs]
Dehydrated Cranberries
[AVOID if diabetic or on blood thinners]
Pomegranate seeds
[AVOID if pregnant or breastfeeding or before surgery]

Chocolate Caliente con Hielo
(Hot Chocolate on Ice)

Mix ingredients well. Pour over crushed ice to serve.
Vanilla almond milk, ¾ cup, heated
Ground Mocha mix, ¼ cup, melted
(Raw coca nibs, carob, dark chocolate)
Ground Cinnamon, 1 TBS
Vanilla extract, 1 tsp
Orange zest, 1 TBS
Maple syrup, 3 TBS

Tommie's Mother's Day Brunch

Llama Lunchwiches

(TOMMIE'S TIP: In keeping with the *Is Your Mamma a Llama?* theme, make Mama sandwiches and child sandwiches for each animal mentioned in the book. Be creative with presentation and cut sandwiches into whimsical or geometric shapes in smaller portions equivalent to ½ a regular-sized sandwich. Make heartier breads into open-faced sandwiches. Children don't like the crusts, so be sure to neatly trim them off before cutting into shapes.)

INGREDIENTS:

BAT SANDWICH 1: (makes 12+/- of each sandwich)
Cream cheese, 16 oz, softened
Black olives, 1 cup, drained, finely chopped
Pepperoni slices, 8 oz package, finely chopped
Salt/pepper, to taste
Ciabatta bread, 12 slices

BAT SANDWICH 2: (makes 12+/- of each sandwich)
Marshmallow fluff, 1 cup
Nutella brand spread, 1 cup
Pretzel rolls, 6 sliced in half

SWAN SANDWICH 1: (makes 12+/- of each sandwich)
Eggs, 12, boiled, chopped
Yogurt, plain, 1 cup
Dill pickle relish, 2 TBS
Sweet pickle relish, 2 TBS
Salt/pepper, to taste
Paprika, for dusting
Brioche buns, 6, halved

SWAN SANDWICH 2: (makes 12+/- of each sandwich)
Chicken breasts, 3, chopped
Mayonnaise, 1 cup
Grapes, green/purple, ½ cup, chopped
Baguettes, 6, halved

COW SANDWICH 1: (makes 12+/- of each sandwich)
Cheddar cheese, sharp, 16 oz, shredded
Yogurt, plain Greek-style, 1 cup
Black olives, ¼ cup, chopped
Pimentos, ¼ cup, chopped
Sugar, granulated, 1 tsp
Salt/pepper, to taste
Potato bread, 12 slices

COW SANDWICH 2: (makes 12+/- of each sandwich)
Cheddar cheese, mild, 16 oz, shredded
Mayonnaise, 1 cup
Green olives, ¼ cup, chopped
Raisins, ¼ cup, chopped
Salt/pepper, to taste
Wonder/white bread, 12 slices

SEAL SANDWICH 1: (makes 12+/- of each sandwich)
Salmon, smoked, 16 oz
Oil, extra virgin olive, 2 TBS
Lemon zest, 3 TBS
Parsley, ½ cup, chopped
Salt/pepper, to taste
French bread, 12 slices, toasted

SEAL SANDWICH 2: (makes 12+/- of each sandwich)
Tuna, 2 large cans, drained
Mayonnaise, ½ cup
Dill pickle, ½ cup, chopped
Salt/pepper, to taste
Raisin bread, 12 slices, toasted

KANGAROO SANDWICH 1: (makes 12+/- of each sandwich)
Garbanzo beans, 2 15-oz cans, drained, mashed
Lemon juice, 1 TBS
Garlic, 2 cloves, minced
Cumin, 1 tsp, ground
Oil, sesame, 1 TBS
Oil, extra virgin olive, 1 TBS
Tomatoes, sun dried in oil, chopped
Pita, 6 pockets, halved

KANGAROO SANDWICH 2: (makes 12+/- of each sandwich)
Peanut butter, 1 cup
Agave syrup, ½ cup
Bananas, 6, sliced
Challah bread, 12 slices

LLAMA SANDWICH 1: (makes 12+/- of each sandwich)
Avocados, 3 large, chopped
Eggs, 6 large, boiled, chopped
Sour cream, 1 cup
Lime zest, 3 TBS
Multigrain bread, 12 slices

LLAMA SANDWICH 2: (makes 12+/- of each sandwich)
Ham, deli-style, 12 slices, chopped
American cheese, 12 slices, chopped
Mustard, 1 tsp
Mayonnaise, 1 tsp
Pickles, hamburger-style dills, ½ cup, chopped
Hawaiian-style sweet rolls, 12

PREPARATION: For each sandwich, combine listed ingredients in a bowl and blend until smooth. Spread mixture evenly on sandwich bread and cut to desired shape.

Llama Lipsmackers

(TOMMIE'S TIP: These are so simple and delicious, it's embarrassing!)
INGREDIENTS:
Cream cheese, 2 8 oz blocks, softened
Pepper jelly, 4 oz jar
(TOMMIE'S TIP: Tommie uses Happy Jalapeno Jelly from Elly's Jelly Jar!)
Berry jam, 4 oz jar
(TOMMIE'S TIP: Tommie uses Triple Berry Jam from Elly's Jelly Jar!)
Tortilla chips
Wheat or cheese crackers
(TOMMIE'S TIP: Quick and easy? Buy from the store.)

PREPARATION: Lay softened cream cheese blocks on two saucers. Spoon pepper jelly over the top of one cheese block and the berry jam over the other. Arrange crackers and chips on matching dinner plates. Set saucers in the middle of the plates. Scoop and eat!

Mama Llama Munchie Mix

INGREDIENTS:
Corn chips, broken
Pretzel sticks, broken in half
Chocolate chips
Golden raisins and/or craisins
Crunchy cereal squares
(TOMMIE'S TIP: Check the cereal aisle in the grocery store for oodles of options!)
Mixed nuts
(TOMMIE'S TIP: For guests with allergies, make up a batch without nuts!)

PREPARATION: Combine equal portions of all ingredients in a large container with a tight lid. Shake gently. Pour into a large punchbowl. Guests may use the ladle to fill punch glasses.
(TOMMIE'S TIP: Another fun presentation is to use large serving bowls and matching teacups, especially if they match the saucer and plates used for the *Llama Lipsmackers!*)

Culinary Creations by Holmes

Even though Finbar Holmes is from Ireland, all ingredients listed are measured in standard United States customary units. Feel free to add, omit, or substitute ingredients.

Boxty with Fried Eggs and Black Pudding

INGREDIENTS: (makes 6-8 cakes)
Potatoes, 8 large, coarsely grated
Onion, 1 medium, chopped
Egg, 1 large, beaten
Salt/pepper, ¼-½ tsp each
Nutmeg, ¼ tsp, grated
Flour, all purpose, 1 TBS
Butter, 3-4 TBS

PREPARATION: Preheat oven to 200°. Line a baking sheet with parchment paper and set inside oven. Grate potatoes into a large bowl lined with a tea towel. Pull up corners of the tea towel to make a sling. Grasp the corners tightly and twist to squeeze as much liquid as possible from the potatoes. (FINBAR SUGGESTS: Use considerable muscle! The boxty needs to be rather dry to crisp up well.) Return to the bowl. Add onion, egg, spices, and flour and mix thoroughly. Melt butter in a large skillet over medium heat. Scoop potato mixture out with a spoon and drop into skillet. Flatten with the back of the spoon into a circular patty. Cook 4 minutes. Flip with a spatula. Cook an additional 4 minutes until boxty cake is golden brown and crispy. Remove to a baking sheet and keep warm in the oven. Serve with fried eggs and black pudding. (FINBAR SUGGESTS: If you don't fancy black pudding or can't find it, use sausage patties.)

Dublin Coddle Casserole

INGREDIENTS: (makes 8 servings)
Oil, vegetable, 2 TBS
Spuds (potatoes), 6, sliced ½" thick
Carrots, 4, sliced into rounds
Salt, 2 tsp
Pepper, 2 tsp
Rashers (thick cut bacon), 1 lb
Bangers (or sausages), 2 lbs
(FINBAR SUGGESTS: A suitable substitute in the States may be kielbasa)
Onions, 2 large, sliced
Chicken broth, 16 oz.
Apple cider vinegar, 2 TBS
Guinness ale, 1 cup
(FINBAR SUGGESTS: Substitute 1 cup broth for those who do not imbibe.)
Parsley, ¼ cup, chopped

PREPARATION: Preheat oven to 325°. Add oil to a large Dutch oven or deep casserole dish. Coat the bottom and use a paper towel to coat the inside walls. Layer the pot so the sliced potatoes are on the bottom. Sprinkle with salt and pepper. Cook the rashers in a deep skillet or pot until crispy. Drain on a paper towel and set aside. Brown the bangers in the rasher drippings until nearly done, but not quite. Set aside with the rashers. Sauté the onions in the remaining fat for about 5 minutes until translucent and beginning to caramelize. Add the broth and vinegar, stirring as it comes to the boil. Remove from the heat and set aside. Crumble the rashers and sprinkle half of them over the top of the potatoes. Carefully pour the broth mixture into the Dutch oven over the potatoes. Add the Guinness. Lay the

bangers atop the lot and set in the oven. Cook covered for one hour. Remove the lid and cook an additional 30-45 minutes uncovered. To serve, ladle into bowls and top with the remaining rashers and chopped parsley. (FINBAR SUGGESTS: *Coddle* goes well with a bit of brown bread and *Kerrygold butter.*)

Matcha Shortbread Biscuits

INGREDIENTS: (makes 25 cookies)
Flour, 2 cups, all purpose
Matcha, 2 TBS + extra for dusting
(FINBAR SUGGESTS: Powdered green tea is NOT suitable. Be sure to use *matcha.*)
Cornstarch, ½ cup
Butter, salted, I cup, softened
(FINBAR SUGGESTS: Don't use the microwave to soften the butter.
Let it occur naturally to room temperature on the countertop.)
Sugar, granulated, 2/3 cup
Sugar, powdered, for dusting

PREPARATION: Preheat oven to 275°. In a large bowl, sift flour, *matcha,* and cornstarch together. In another bowl, cream butter and sugar until smooth and fluffy. Add flour mixture and combine to form a dough. Line a baking sheet with parchment paper. Press dough onto the baking sheet. Prick the surface of each cookie all over with a fork. Bake for ½ hour. Reduce heat to 250° and continue baking for I hour until edges of cookies are beginning to turn golden brown. Remove from oven and cool on a wire rack. Cut into 25 rectangles whilst still warm. Dust with powdered sugar and *matcha.*

Tamale Pie

INGREDIENTS: (makes 8 servings)

Butter, ½ cup unsalted
Cornmeal, 1 cup fine
Eggs, 2 large
Honey, 2 TBS
Buttermilk, 1 ½ cups
Flour, 1 cup self-rising
Creamed corn, ½ cup
Olive oil, 1 TBS
Green onion, ½ cup chopped
Chili powder, 1 tsp
Salt & pepper, to taste
Garlic, 2 cloves minced
Ground beef, 1 lb
Easy Enchilada Sauce (FINBAR SUGGESTS: Use Thomasina's recipe),
1/3 cup
Black olives, 1 small can, sliced
Cheddar Jack cheese, 2 cups
Cilantro, 1 TBS chopped
Sour cream, for serving

PREPARATION—CORNBREAD: Melt butter in a deep cast-iron skillet. (FINBAR SUGGESTS: A glass or nonstick oven-safe pan will work; however, cast iron will yield the best result!) Set aside. In large bowl, combine cornmeal, salt, honey, eggs, buttermilk, and creamed corn. Add flour and ½ the butter. Whisk. Pour batter into the remaining butter in the skillet. Place in a preheated 400° oven and bake for 25 minutes.

PREPARATION—BEEF MIXTURE: In another skillet, heat oil over medium heat. Add onion and chili powder and cook until softened, about 5 minutes. Add garlic and cook 1 minute longer. Add ground beef and cook until done, about 6 minutes. Drain fat. Season with salt and pepper to taste.

PREPARATION—TAMALE PIE: Poke entire surface of cornbread (in the skillet) with a fork. Top with *Easy Enchilada Sauce*. Add beef mixture and top with olives and cheese. Cover

with foil and bake in 400° oven for 20 minutes. Remove foil and broil until cheese bubbles, about 5 minutes. Garnish with cilantro and serve with sour cream. (FINBAR SUGGESTS: Cut the pie in squares. Use a wide spatula to get cleanly under the cornbread crust.)

Mexican Flan

INGREDIENTS: (makes 8 servings)
Sweetened condensed milk, 1 can
Evaporated milk, 1 can
Eggs, 6
Cream cheese, 8 oz package
Vanilla, 1 tsp
Water, 2 TBS
Sugar, 1 cup

PREPARATION: In a medium-sized saucepan, bring sugar and water to a boil over high heat until sugar dissolves. Reduce heat and continue boiling about 10 minutes until syrup is a light brown color. Pour into an oven proof pan, tilting the pan until the caramel covers the bottom evenly. Let cool. Place the remaining ingredients in a bowl and beat until the mixture is smooth. Slowly pour over the caramel and cover with aluminum foil. Place the pan inside a large baking pan. Add warm water to the outer pan until it is about ¾ inch deep. Bake in 325° oven for no more than 50 minutes. Remove from oven and let it cool. Once cooled, run a sharp knife between the flan and the baking pan to release it. Place a large pie plate or serving dish on top of the pan and quickly invert. (FINBAR SUGGESTS: Use care to avoid spilling liquid caramel.) Slice and serve.

Mexican Coffee

INGREDIENTS: (makes 4 servings)
Coffee beans, ¾ cup ground
(FINBAR SUGGESTS: Dark roast is quite decadent!)

Water, 5 cups
Cinnamon, 2 tsp ground
Heavy cream, ½ cup
Whole milk, ½ cup
Dark brown sugar, 2 TBS
Orange rind, 1 grated
Chocolate, 3 oz semisweet dark
Vanilla, 1 tsp

PREPARATION: Place ground coffee beans and cinnamon in coffee filter in coffee pot and brew with the water. Let sit 3-4 minutes. In a saucepan, place cream, milk, orange peel, chocolate, and brown sugar. Pour brewed coffee into pan and heat over low 5-10 minutes, stirring constantly until sugar and cholate melt. Remove from heat and strain out orange peel. Whisk in vanilla. To serve, pour into cups. Top with a splash of cream and a sprinkle of cinnamon. (FINBAR SUGGESTS: Whipped cream or vanilla ice cream are lovely toppings!)

Cinco de Mayo Celebration Street Vendor Foods

Chips de Tortilla Fritos
<u>FRIED TORTILLA CHIPS</u>
(*Cabina I* - Leon Luz)
INGREDIENTS:
Flour, 3 cups (all purpose, plain white, bread,
or authentic Mexican *El Rosal*)
Baking powder, I tsp
Salt, I tsp
Water, I cup, hot
Oil, vegetable, I/3 cup

PREPARATION - TORTILLAS: In a large bowl, whisk together flour, baking powder, and salt. Make a well in the center. Add water and vegetable oil. Mix with hands to bring the dough together so it is still sticky to the touch. Sprinkle the top of the dough and dust hands with a little extra flour if too sticky. Turn dough out onto a lightly floured work surface. Knead to form a smooth, soft ball, about 2-3 minutes. Divide dough into 16 equal balls. Flatten one ball out with hands to make a circle. Lightly dust both sides with flour and set aside. Cover with a tea towel for 10 minutes. Heat a nonstick pan over medium-high heat. Using a rolling pin, flatten one tortilla to a 6-inch circle about ¼-inch thick. To avoid drying out, work with only one tortilla at a time. Cook the tortilla in skillet until golden with a few brown spots, about 1-2 minutes. Flip and continue cooking an additional 30 seconds until more spots appear. While one tortilla is cooking, roll the next one out and repeat steps. Stack them up on a plate lined with a

clean tea towel and wrap them up to keep them warm and soft while cooking the rest.

PREPARATION - CHIPS: Heat 1-inch of oil in a large frying pan over medium-high heat (about 350 °F.) Stack the tortillas and cut into 8 equal wedges. Fry a few chips at a time, turning occasionally until chips are crispy and lightly browned, about 1 minute. Drain chips on paper towels or flattened brown paper sacks. Sprinkle lightly with salt

Queso Fundido Picante Salsa
SPICY HOT MELTED CHEESE SAUCE
(*Cabina 3* - Letitia Luz)
INGREDIENTS:
White cheese (Manchego, white American, white Velveeta, or Monterrey Jack) 2 lbs, cubed
Heavy cream, 1 cup
Tomato, 1 cup, finely chopped
Jalapeño peppers, 1 cup, seeded and chopped
Habanero peppers, 1 cup, seeded and chopped
Tabasco sauce, 1 cup
Cilantro, ½ cup, chopped
Onion, 2 large, chopped

PREPARATION: Melt cheese and heavy cream in a large saucepan over medium-low heat, until smooth. Stir in tomato, peppers, onions, and cilantro. Keep warm in a CrockPot or slow cooker on LOW. Serve with tortilla chips.

Salsa Roja Sedosa
JO'S SILKY RED SAUCE
(*Cabina 5* - Susan Clay)
INGREDIENTS:
Tomatoes, 5 large, halved

Onion, I large, quartered
Serrano chiles, 2, stemmed, chopped
Garlic, 2 cloves, crushed
Oil, vegetable, 2 TBS
Water, 4 cups
Cilantro, 12 stalks, chopped
Salt, I tsp + salt to taste

PREPARATION: Put all ingredients except cilantro and salt into a pot. Cover with water by I". Bring to a boil. Reduce heat and simmer 20-30 minutes. Remove from heat. Add cilantro and salt. Blend until smooth. Add oil to a deep Dutch oven and heat on low-medium. Pour blended salsa into the pot and simmer 20 minutes until reduced and thickened. Season with additional salt to taste.

Salsa en Capas
ELLY'S LAYERED SAUCE
(*Cabina 5* - Elaine Frank)
INGREDIENTS: (makes 48 jars)
Refried beans, 3-15 oz cans
Avocado, 4 large, mashed
Lime, 2, juiced
Goya *Pico de Gallo* sauce, 17.6 oz jar
Sour cream, 2 cups
Cacique Queso Fresco, 2 cups, crumbled

PREPARATION: Layer ingredients in ¼ pint quilted jelly jars in the following order: beans, avocado + lime, *pico de gallo* sauce, sour cream, and topped with crumbled cheese. Secure lid and eat with a spoon.

Pico de Gallo Fresco

FRESH PICO DE GALLO
(*Cabina 7* - Lara Padilla)
INGREDIENTS: (makes 12 cups)
Tomatoes, 9 large
Cilantro, 1 cup, chopped
Coriander leaves, 1cup, chopped
White onion, 1 cup, minced
Jalapeño or serrano chili, ½ cup, chopped
Lime juice, 6 TBS
Salt, 2 tsp

PREPARATION: Cut tomatoes in half. Scoop out seeds and watery center. Dice to ¼" size. In a bowl, combine tomatoes and the remaining ingredients except salt and lime juice. Cover and chill in the refrigerator. Add salt and lime juice just before serving.

Infusiones y Remedios de Hierbas

HERBAL TEAS & REMEDIES
(*Cabina 9* - Gertrudis Padilla)

Para el Vientre –
Indigestión, Náuseas, o Dolor de Estómago
(FOR THE BELLY –
INDIGESTION, NAUSEA, OR STOMACHACHE)
- Drink ½ cup Celery juice with 1 tsp olive oil
- Chew raw papaya pulp and dried orange peel
- Drink lemon/lime juice in warm water with honey

Para la Cabeza –
Embriaguez, Resaca, o Dolor de Cabeza

(FOR THE HEAD –
DRUNKENNESS, HANGOVER, OR HEADACHE)
- Rosemary/white willow tincture
- Lavender/lemon balm tincture
- Basil/chamomile tincture

Para el Corazón –
Acidez o Reflujo Ácido,
(FOR THE HEART –
HEARTBURN OR ACID REFLUX)
- Drink passionflower tea
- Sip ½ cup boiled marshmallow root with licorice
- Drink 2 tsp apple cider vinegar, 1 TBS raw honey,
in ½ cup warm water.
- Swallow 10 drops peppermint leaf, basil leaf, and parsley
tincture (given to Dr. Frank)

Tamales Carnitas Flores
FLORES PORK TAMALES
(*Cabina 11* - Hector & Carmine Flores)
INGREDIENTS: (makes 24)
CARNITAS:
Pork butt, 6 lbs, trimmed, cubed
Oil, 4 TBS
Garlic, 1 tsp, minced
Salt, 4 TBS
Cumin, 2 tsp
Smoked paprika, 2 tsp
Chili powder, 4 tsp
Onion, 1, chopped
Jalapeño chili pepper, 1, seeded, chopped
ENCHILADA SAUCE:
Tomato sauce, 2 8-oz cans
Flour, all purpose, 6 TBS

TAMALES:
Corn husks, 24 large, dried
MASA DOUGH:
Masa harina, 6 cups
Salt, 1 tsp
Baking powder, 2 tsp
Oil, vegetable, 1 cup
Broth or water, 3-4 cups

PREPARATION – PORK CARNITAS: Combine spices in a small bowl and mix well. Place pork in a large bowl and sprinkle with seasoning mix, coating each piece. Save ¼ of the mixture for later. Heat oil in a deep Dutch oven to high. Brown the coated pork about 5 minutes on each side. Add onion, chili pepper, and water to cover pork by 1" and reduce heat. Simmer uncovered, checking water level often. When the liquid is reduced by half, add more water to cover the pork. Cook for 1 ½ to 2 hours, until pork can be easily pulled into strips with two forks but doesn't fall apart. Remove pork and let it rest until cooled. Pull the pork into bite-sized strips with hands.

PREPARATION – ENCHILADA SAUCE: Add tomato sauce to the remaining liquid in the Dutch oven, along with the reserved ¼ of the seasoning mixture and mix to combine. Simmer on medium heat. Thicken with flour mixed with water to make it smooth. Add to liquid slowly, stirring constantly until thickened. Return pork to the large mixing bowl and coat with half of the enchilada sauce.

PREPARATION – MASA DOUGH: Combine masa harina, baking powder, and salt in a large bowl. Add oil and mix together with hands. Add broth little by little, mixing with hands until the dough is soft and spreadable.

PREPARATION – TAMALES: Soak corn husks in warm water to rehydrate and soften, about 20 minutes. Spread masa dough on top half of the corn husk to about half the thickness of the little fingertip. Add ¼ cup pork along the center. Fold the tamale in

half lengthwise, making sure the seams on the side meet evenly in the middle. Fold the bottom half to meet the top. Tie a thin strip of corn husk around the center of the tamale to keep it closed. Place folded tamales in a steamer basket over a large pot of boiling water. Steam for 45-60 minutes until a toothpick inserted in the center comes out clean. Remove and let cool. Tamales may be served immediately or refrigerated to serve the next day. Drizzle with remaining enchilada sauce or use for dipping.

Empanadas de Pollo

CHICKEN EMPANADAS
(*Cabina 13* - Ladies of *Iglesia de Santa Maria*)
INGREDIENTS: (makes 24)
DOUGH:
Flour, all purpose, 6 cups
Salt, 2 tsp
Baking powder, 1 tsp
Baking soda, 1 tsp
Water, 2 cups, warm
Oil, vegetable, ½ cup
FILLING:
Oil, vegetable, 4 TBS
Chicken, 2 lbs, cooked, shredded
Onion, 1, diced
Olives, ½ cup green, sliced
Cilantro, fresh, ½ cup, chopped
Garlic, 2 cloves, crushed
Tomato paste, 2 TBS
Paprika, 1 tsp
Cumin, 1 tsp
Chili powder, ½ tsp
Sugar, 2 TBS
Salt/black pepper, to taste

Oil, vegetable, for frying

PREPARATION - DOUGH: In a large bowl, mix flour, salt, baking powder, and baking soda. Add water and ½ cup oil. Mix well with hands and form a dough. Knead on lightly floured surface for 2-3 minutes. Divide in half. Cover with plastic wrap or tea towels and set aside.

PREPARATION – FILLING: Heat 4 TBS oil in a large skillet over medium to medium-high heat. Sauté shredded chicken with remaining filling ingredients until heated through, about 10-12 minutes. Remove from heat and cool.

PREPARATION – EMPANADAS: Divide dough into 24 equal balls and press each into a 4-inch circle. Place 2 TBS filling in the center of each circle. Carefully fold dough over filling into half-moon shape, making sure ends meet. Lightly dampen inside of seam with a fingertip dipped in water. Press edges together with a fork to seal, making sure no filling is trapped in the seam. Heat 1 cup oil in large skillet over medium heat. Fry empanadas in hot oil about 5 minutes per side, turning once. Add more oil for frying if necessary. Drain on paper towels or flattened out brown paper sacks.

Refrescos Fríos

COLD SOFT DRINKS
(*Cabina 15* - Ladies of *Iglesia de Santa María*)
Coca Cola, Pepsi, *Jarritos* Fruit Sodas, Fanta Orange, Fanta Pineapple, *Jupi* Fruit Sodas

Caramelos de Tamarindo

TAMARIND CANDIES
(*Cabina 2* - Padre Juan Sanchez)
Pulparindo, Tama Roca Banderilla, Pelon Mini, Rellerindos

Platanos con Lechera
FRIED BANANAS IN SWEET MILK
(*Cabina 4* - Finbar Holmes)
INGREDIENTS: (makes 24 servings)
Bananas, 12 large (7 ½ lbs)
Cinnamon, ground, 6 TBS
Butter, 6 TBS (FINBAR SUGGESTS: Use real butter, not margarine!)
Sweetened condensed milk, 3 6-oz cans
(FINBAR SUGGESTS: Nestle's La Léche and Borden's Eagle Brand are both good.)

PREPARATION: Peel and slice bananas in half, then in half lengthwise. Sprinkle with ground cinnamon. Melt butter in a large skillet over medium heat. Place bananas in skillet, cinnamon side up. Cook 2-3 minutes. Flip and cook 2-3 minutes on the other side until golden brown. Place 2 slices on a plate and drizzle with the milk. Serve whilst warm.

Carne Seca de Alvarez
BEEF JERKY OR "DRY MEAT"
(*Cabina 6* - Don Lareby)
INGREDIENTS: (makes 24 servings)
Chuck roast, 7 lbs
Water, to cover roast
Onions, 2 large, chopped
Garlic, 2 cloves, minced
Cumin, 1 tsp, ground
Green chili salsa, 1 28-oz can
Salt/pepper, to taste
Flour tortillas, 12, 6-inch

PREPARATION: Heat oven to 250°. Place raw meat in a large roasting pan. Cover with water by 1". Add remaining ingredients, except tortillas, salt, and pepper. Cover pan. Roast overnight. The next morning, drain the meat. Reserve the broth but discard

onion and garlic. Cool meat for an hour. Shred meat with hands, pulling with the grain. Discard fat, bone, and gristle. In a large bowl, combine shredded meat with salsa to marinate. Cover with cling film and set bowl in refrigerator overnight. The next morning, fill a Dutch oven with meat and enough broth to fill the pot halfway. Simmer, uncovered, until most of the liquid has evaporated. Season with salt and pepper to taste. Keep warm in an aluminum foil-covered bowl. Serve with tortillas cut in wedges.

Elotes en Brochetas

<u>CORN ON SKEWERS</u>
(*Cabina 6* - Henry Erving)
INGREDIENTS: (makes 24)
Corn on the cob, 24 whole
Lime juice, 6 tsp
Salt, 6 tsp + 2 tsps
Mayonnaise, 3 cups
Queso Fresco cheese, crumbled, 4 cups
Chili powder, 1 ½ cups (or paprika)

PREPARATION: Fill a large cookpot with water. Add 2 tsps salt and bring to a boil. Add corn and cook for 5-10 minutes. Remove corn and sprinkle with lime juice and remaining salt. Skewer each corn cob. Spread mayonnaise over the entire surface. Grate/crumble cheese into a shallow plate. Roll the corn in the cheese, then sprinkle with chili powder to serve.

Dos Más Dos Taquitos

<u>TWO PLUS TWO TAQUITOS</u>
(*Cabina 8* - Tommie Watson)

Cerdo con Queso

CHEESY PULLED PORK
INGREDIENTS: (makes 36)
Pork shoulder or Boston butt, 3 cups pulled
(TOMMIE'S TIP: Cook the pork shoulder/Boston butt in the CrockPot the day before.)
Oaxaca cheese, 3 cups, shredded
(TOMMIE'S TIP: Try *La Morenita* or *Ole Mexican Verole.*)
Salsa, 1 cup
(TOMMIE'S TIP: Mateo's and Pace are good, but I like Newman's Own!)
Oil, coconut, 4-5 tsp on paper towel
Corn tortillas, 36

PREPARATION: Preheat oven to 400°. Heat a griddle or non-stick skillet over medium-high heat. In a bowl, combine pulled pork, cheese, and salsa. Set aside. Rub a bit of coconut oil onto one side of each tortilla. Place tortilla flat on griddle/skillet for about 30 seconds until it just begins to brown. Remove and lay on paper towels. Continue until all tortillas are warmed. Spread 1 TBS pork, cheese, and salsa mixture evenly over each tortilla. Quickly roll into a tight tube and place, seam side down, on a foil-lined baking sheet. Bake 12 minutes until shells are crunchy. Keep warm by covering tightly with paper towels and foil. (TOMMIE'S TIP: Don't tent the foil. It will create steam and ruin that crunchiness!) Serve with sour cream.

Pollo con Salsa Verde
CHICKEN WITH GREEN SAUCE
INGREDIENTS: (makes 24)
Chicken, 8 cups, shredded
(TOMMIE'S TIP: Rotisserie chickens work great!)
Salsa Verde, 2 cups prepared
(TOMMIE'S TIP: *Herdez,* Pace, and *El Mexicano* are all good brands!)
Cacique Queso quesadilla cheese, ½ cup shredded
(TOMMIE'S TIP: *Cacique* is best, but Walmart's Great Value is also tasty!)
Avocado, 4 large, mashed
Lime, 4 large, juiced
Cilantro, ¼ cup, chopped

Flour tortillas, 24

PREPARATION: Preheat oven to 400°. In a bowl, mix chicken, *salsa verde,* and cheese. Set aside. Heat a griddle or non-stick skillet over medium-high heat. In a small bowl, combine avocado, lime juice, and cilantro. Set aside. Place tortilla flat on griddle/skillet for about 30 seconds until it just begins to brown. Remove and lay on paper towels. Continue until all tortillas are warmed. Spread 1 TBS chicken, cheese, and *salsa verde* mixture evenly over each tortilla. Quickly roll into a tight tube and place, seam side down, on a parchment paper-lined baking sheet. Bake 7 minutes. Turn shells. Bake 5 more minutes. Turn shells. Bake 2 more minutes until shells are crunchy. (TOMMIE'S TIP: Don't worry if some filling escapes. That's normal.) Keep warm by covering tightly with paper towels and foil. (TOMMIE'S TIP: Don't tent the foil. It will create steam and ruin that crunchiness!) Serve with avocado mixture.

Sopes de Ternera con Frijoles Negros
BEEF TORTILLAS WITH BLACK BEANS
(*Cabina 10* - Jorge/Soledad Fuentes)
INGREDIENTS: (MAKES 24)
Masa harina, 2 cups
Water, 3 cups, warm
Oil, vegetable, 1 cup +1 tsp
Salsa, 2 cups
Black beans, 2 cups
Beef, 2 cups, shredded
Cotija cheese, 1 cup, crumbled
Avocado, 4, mashed
Mexican crema or sour cream, ½ cup

Preparation: Combine masa, salt, and 2/3 cup warm water in a large bowl. Stir with a wooden spoon until it becomes a soft dough. Add a little more water, if needed, to make it smooth but

not sticky. With hands, shape into 1 ½-inch balls and cover with a tea towel to avoid drying out. With hands, flatten each ball into a ¼-inch thick circle. Heat a large cast-iron skillet over medium-high heat. When the skillet is hot, lay the *sopes* in the dry skillet and toast until brown spots appear, about 30 seconds to 2 minutes per side. Transfer *sopes* to a baking sheet. Pinch the sides to form a rim while they are still hot. Cover with tea towel to avoid drying out. Heat the oil in the skillet over medium-high heat. Fry *sopes* until golden brown, about 1-2 minutes. Flip the *sopes* over and fry the other sides, about 1-2 minutes. Carefully remove the *sopes* and drain on paper towels or flattened brown paper bags. Spoon salsa into the center of each shell. Top with a layer of beans, shredded beef, *cotija* cheese, avocado, and crema.

Churros de Canela

CINNAMON CHURROS

(*Cabina 12* - Men of *Iglesia de Santa Maria*)
INGREDIENTS: (makes 24)
Water, 2 cups
Vanilla extract, 2 tsp
Salt, ¼ tsp
Butter, 4 TBS
Flour, 2 cups, sifted twice
Eggs, 2 large, beaten
Oil, vegetable, 5 cups, for frying
Sugar, to dust
Cinnamon, ground, 1 tsp, to dust

PREPARATION: Preheat the oil in a cast iron skillet or Dutch oven to 320°. (Use a candy thermometer). Combine water, vanilla extract, salt, and butter in a deep saucepan over medium-high heat. Bring to a rolling boil. Stir in the flour all at once to boiling water. Mix with a wooden spoon very quickly to incorporate the flour. Remove the pan from the heat and let it

rest I minute. Add egg. Mix until completely incorporated into the dough. Keep mixing until it is smooth and soft and separates from the bottom of the pot. Spoon the dough into a pastry bag fitted with a star-shaped tip. Pipe 6-inch strips directly into the hot oil, cutting them off with sharp scissors. *CAUTION: DO NOT TOUCH THE OIL OR THE CHURROS WHILE THEY ARE FIRST FRYING! THEY WILL POP AND SPLATTER!* Fry for 2-3 minutes until golden brown on one side. Carefully and quickly, flip the churro over with a wooden spoon or stick. Fry for 2 more minutes. Remove from the oil and drain on paper towels or flattened brown paper bags. Roll in sugar, and sprinkle with cinnamon.

Cervezas Heladas
ICED BEER
(*Cabina 14* - Men of *Iglesia de Santa Maria*)
Corona, Modelo, Pacifico, Tecate, Dos Equis

About the Author

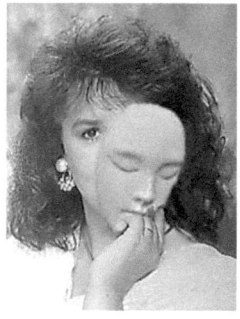

MICHELLE BUSBY is a Florida transplant who lived for a time in California where she was an actress, singer, and writer and a member of the American Federation of Television and Radio Artists (AFTRA). A life-long thespian and former teacher, she has performed on stage since her teens and has written plays, musicals, and novels for all ages under the pen names of Mickey MorningGlory, Mickey Middleton, and M.M. Busby. An avid puzzle solver, mystery buff, and self-proclaimed foodie, she combines her talents into one large pot where she stews up her Holmes and Watson Culinary Whodunits. She is a member of *Sisters in Crime (SinC), Women's Fiction Writers Association (WFWA), National Association of Independent Writers and Editors (NAIWE), American Copy Editors Society (ACES), and Society of Children's Book Writers and Illustrators (SCBWI).* Michelle lives in Florida with her family.

Readers can visit Michelle at patentprintbks.com.